EDDIE KRUMBLE IS
THE CLAPPER

EDDIE KRUMBLE IS
THE CLAPPER

Dito Montiel

Thunder's Mouth Press
New York

My name is Edward Krumble. Sounds like a joke huh? Yeah, I know. Yeah, I like to say "well" a lot. Not so much that I like to, just do I guess. At least in the beginning. When I'm nervous, like before we get to know each other. Fact I seldom get to know many people it can go on a while. Who cares right? I mean, what words I like or don't like to say.

Well, I often say well. Could probably end this whole story right here if it weren't for the past six months. Really. I mean, that woulda been it. My name is Edward Krumble and I like to say well a lot. What a novel. Fascinating. Short. To the point, no big payoff and . . . yeah.

I was born and raised in Queens, New York. Moved out here (Los Angeles) in the early '90s because well . . . (I'm cutting back) I did. Simple as that. New York was HELL at the time and I saw a cardboard cutout in a Forest Hills subway station that had a picture of a palm tree and thought . . . *OK*.

Believe it was a Bacardi ad. Probably Palo Viejo (the old tree) or something. Maybe some Club Med getaway deal thing. I don't know. Pretty funny, my whole life was turned around, or better said, continued 3,000 miles away on account of a subway ad I can't recall. For that matter, if it was even Los Angeles the ad was depicting. Ugh, hate running out of words and using ones like "depicting." Yeah, I just "quoted" myself as well. Hate that, too.

I'm not a hateful guy, just sometimes a bit stressed. I have to stop that.

Come to think of it, that ad was probably of Puerto Rico. Being Bacardi and all. The palm tree was probably a coconut one or something.

Anyway, here I am and not to any credit, hard work, or even determination does this story get any more interesting. It all just happened.

Co-op

In New York I worked one awful job after another. Too many to recall. Let's just say I worked in a lock MAKING factory, OK. Idea that someone actually MADE locks never even occurred to me. Like ketchup, toilet paper, and nightmares these things do have places of origin. Methods of conception. Poor schmuck somewhere's gotta put those metal attachments holding erasers to pencils, right? Another's gotta make sure MEDECO locks go in Medeco boxes. That someone was often me.

Did you know in 1968, the owners and employees of MEDECO developed a **unique locking principle of angled key cuts and elevating and rotating pin tumblers that provided millions of key combinations and a level of security unmatched in its time?**

Of course not. I do because I worked in a LOCK FACTORY. Horrible. At one time I even knew what that meant. It was in Long Island City, Queens, and appropriately had no windows.

I was a kid, and being the teachers in my high school predicted an absolute and virtually BLEAK future for me, they recommended a program called Co-op.

Seems they (the teachers) would have meetings discussing the non-futures (lack thereof) in a bunch of us. Once unanimously decided upon what kids had absolutely no chance of becoming or contributing anything, they would recommend Co-op. One week school, one week work. Designed to help prepare or ease you into a long menial existence in such desirable fields as mailroom department maintenance clerk (guy who CLEANS the Zig-Zag papers off the floor after the messengers go home from hard days of getting high and licking stamps).

Either way, one week school, one week work sounded like a good deal to me. Hated them both but this would cut each in half (I do sometimes see the glass half full).

My father couldn't of been more happy. Trading in my ENTIRE FUTURE for a list of such promising careers as: the "up-and-comer" at the dimly lit DMV (department of motor vehicles) located right INSIDE the Queensbridge Projects (murder capital of New York at the time), the negligently-discarded-hypodermic-needle collector of Rockaway Beach, and well, the factory opportunities were endless.

Getting a job was a cinch as only one other program competed with Co-op at the remedial wages offered for these pristine opportunities. That program being work release for convicted felons.

Once chosen to be a part of this (failed experiment), you and your parents had to sign a consent form.

They'd convince (see "trickery" in the dictionary) them (your parents) by assuring not only would you be receiving a top-notch education, but an understanding of the working world you were soon to be thrust into. All this while generating a little extra spending money. Great deal.

When you'd come in (student/guinea pig) they'd have you fill out a request form. What kind of jobs would you find most fulfilling? Well, I'd LOVE to work in a record shop, guitar store, even a roller-skating rink. Hey, this seems like a great idea.

They'd accept your form, shake hands with your parents, and off you went to toilet maintenance at the local public restrooms (homosexual copulation grounds) in the park. Astoria Park to be precise.

Watching the kids being handed their newly assigned places of employment can best be compared to that of families walking in and out of all-you-can-eat restaurants. Much happier entering than exiting.

The Lock-Factory Kid

As mentioned, my career pendulum landed on the coveted LOCK FACTORY kid.

I'd be that young breath of fresh air in the warehouse. The promising new pony at the track. Did I mention there were no windows?

Hell on earth. Well, I shouldn't say that. The guys I worked with were nice.

It changed on a dime for me one spring. There was an older guy there, Steve. Always looking out for me. Teaching me how to make keys, differences between certain locks. Strange how these things can actually begin to interest you after a while. Full of facts about locks and keys. A walking *Britannica* on it.

Steve was about as relatively normal a guy as you could imagine.

Aside from one strange comment he confided in me about how "two rolls of electrical tape and one Kryptonite (lock) could easily restrain three grown humans silently behind a two-foot closet space for a lifetime if they **deserved** it." Well, of course, why else would we wanna do such a thing? Yeesh. Besides that (he only mentioned that once) Steve was as normal as they came . . . in a lock-making factory.

Anyway, it was spring and he took me aside. "Ya know, Edward, we all love you here and summer's coming. You'll be able to work full time, save up, maybe even get yourself a car or something."

My recollection of that conversation actually ended as he muttered the words SUMMER and FULL TIME through his cigarette-clenched teeth in the same paragraph. All of a sudden reality hit me. I was working in a LOCK FACTORY!

They sent me on a delivery (my favorite because I actually got to see daylight). Went directly to a pay phone, called my friend Chris and decided we needed to run away to California.

Chris's last name is Plork. Chris Plork. Yeah. He was always a little overweight so, needless to say, the whole school experience was a nightmare for him as well.

Over the years we'd both come to the conclusion: never trust a person who had a pleasurable grade school experience.

Chris was messy, lazy, and disliked almost all the same things I did. We became lifelong friends in the very forgettable adventures of the mundane. He, I, and a midget (small person) nicknamed Puppet were the only white kids in Co-op at our high school.

Puppet was, well everyone was racist at the time, but Puppet was quite vocal about it. This made mine and Chris's life a COMPLETE hell on school weeks. Puppet was a dungaree-wearing/cutoff-fringed-sleeves, Neil-Young-painted-on-the-back-of-his-jacket (*Rust Never Sleeps*), pot-smoking, angry-white-teenage little person. DISCO SUCKS! and FUCK IRAN button wearing, *High Times*–reading, racial-slur-spewing machine.

He worked on his off weeks with Mike Murphy. Oh yeah, four white kids. Murphy was kinda forgettable cuz, well, he slept through every single class. ALWAYS! No joke. You almost had to admire his level of defiance. Defiance may not be the right word. More like, could-give-a-damnance.

Murphy could care LESS what anyone did or said. He'd walk into first period, put his head down and never pick it up til he went home. Never. And far as I know, that is the beginning and end of his story.

On school weeks we (the Co-op family) had ALL our classes together, in the same classroom, continuously, without a lunch period. Crazy, right? This conveniently allowed the school to follow through with its ongoing curriculum, exerting as little time and energy into the wasteful thought of teaching us ANY-THING. Us, busy doing drugs, cutting classes, inciting race riots, and sleeping, just happened to fit perfectly into this curriculum. So it all worked out you see.

I learned three things in high school. William Henry Harrison was the shortest-term president in United States history (why that stuck I'll never know), Mike Murphy will NOT wake up if you yell "fire" in an uninterested classroom, and if a white midget yells "nigger" in a predominantly black school the next tallest white kid will get their face punched in.

Puppet and Mike Murphy worked at a steel mine in Queens.

Thypin Steel. Didn't even know one existed in New York but leave it to Co-op to find that diamond in the rough.

At first I thought they made the place up (a lot of us never worked and had friends sign papers to fake jobs). Eventually believed them as they'd proudly go on and on about how the ASBESTOS ROOM (yup) paid triple-time for teenagers. It was all very *Norma Rae*–ish. *Norma Rae* meets inner-city *Rock 'n' Roll High School,* if you can picture it.

So back at my LOCK JOB they used those two words . . . summer and FULL TIME. My friend Chris was gonna meet me on my break and off we were headed to California.

According to Co-op he was employed at FUNGU'S bakery in Jackson Heights (ask an Italian). A fictitious place we made up so he could sit in his basement all day and smoke pot. I was signing the papers and he was a great worker. *Mr. Italian* was his boss's and my surname. Pretty original huh?

Chris lived with his grandmother who suffered so bad from Alzheimer's she used to actually tell me he (Chris) was DEAD (no joke)!

He'd steal his weekly twenty dollars from her purse, eat a meal with her, and retreat directly back to his black-lit basement full of rock posters to smoke pot. Perfect . . . . ly awful. Yes.

Grandma never seemed to mind, and if anything, quite enjoyed sharing an occasional breakfast, lunch, and/or dinner with the corpse of her dead grandson. So this all worked out as well.

I told Chris on the phone about the words they used (SUMMER/FULL TIME). He, of course, like me, saw the tragedy in them and agreed it was probably a good time to run away to Los Angeles. Well, I kinda pushed for it and he was like . . . yeah, sure.

Bleak no sugar.

Plan was simple. Take my lunch. Meet Chris. Hop a Greyhound to Los Angeles. Never come back.

Nothing too dramatic.

On my way out, Steve (the nice older guy at the job) gave me a dollar and asked if I'd grab him a coffee on my way back. I felt bad. Didn't wanna steal the guy's dollar but I was outta there.

"Black no sugar, right Eddie?" I was so out of it I actually thought he asked for a coffee "bleak no future." I hesitated, then realized what he said.

Grabbed him a coffee and brought it right back. "Hey, you *coulda* brought it after ya ate." But I was gone.

Me and Chris went to the 42nd Street bus depot with $270 between us. Two hundred from his grandmother's purse and seventy I had saved from the lock gig. One way or round trip was $39.

Because we were teenagers they wanted a reason why, on a school day, two high school students were buying one-way tickets clear across the country.

Felt like a hostage wanting to carve out *"because they're trying to keep me in a lock factory for summer,"* as they called some police over and we ran. Abandoning our plan.

On our train ride back to Queens I thought of a joke my mother used to tell. Well, she considered it a joke. I saw it as a sort of half story. About a seven-year-old who stands on a corner holding a suitcase. Woman comes up. Asks him what he's doing. "I'm running away but I'm not allowed to cross the street." She thought that joke was so funny. I never did, and certainly didn't on this day.

When I got home my father was furious. "Job called. Said you went to lunch and never came back."

Had to think quick.

Words are so strong. Their power is incredible. Chris, in a moment of clarity, once actually found the answer to racism in a word. If someone would find one harsh enough to equal "nigger" for white people, it would all be over. "Long as 'honky' is the best they can do we'll never stop with that shit." I found that observation incredible. He has no recollection of it.

The word with that kind of strength in my house was "stupid." My father HATED that word. If I was gonna get outta this, "stupid" held the key.

"Every day I show up for work at that lock company this old guy there Steve calls me stupid!"

Couldn't believe I said that. Actually just blurted right outta me. My father went off!

Picked up the phone and threatened poor old Steve's LIFE.

"Playing innocent gives me a good mind to show up there and ring your goddamned neck!" After he hung up I was ordered to go in the morning and pick up my last check. "You show that bastard just how *stupid* you are when you go pick up that last check they owe you and march the hell outta there!"

There was no way I was gonna do this. Felt awful. Poor old Steve was probably shivering in his boots.

Morning came and I went straight to Chris's basement (FUNGU'S BAKERY).

Chris's basement/Fungu's bakery. (and if your grandmother is dead, how is she talking to us?)

My recollection of Chris's basement begins and ends with Led Zeppelin blasting amidst black-light posters as he would sit motionless smoking his brains out. In time, the only movement he'd make became so minuscule, minute, you'd have to be staring intently to know it actually occurred.

When that upbeat part of "Dazed and Confused" would kick in he'd immeasurably nod a half "yeah, I like this part." I'd take note. A sign he's still half alive, or half dead (my position on this varied). Remarkable. Captivating. No.

I'm convinced if I didn't initiate conversation from time to time we'd probably go months without a word being uttered. He wouldn't find this strange at all. Not one bit.

I once watched him smoke joint after joint, no music on, no TV, no nothing, for almost two straight hours. Staring right at me. Almost through me. Complete silence. Minimal blinks. Just waiting for a single word to be said. I purposely didn't play any music wondering when he'd eventually break down and at least ask I put something on. Say something. Anything. Two full hours into it he finally muttered an uncontested, "yeah, I don't know, ya know," got up, and sat back down in silence.

I go back and forth with who's more crazy. Fact that I don't even smoke pot always gave me cause for concern.

Since I moved in, Grandma isn't sure . . . well, was gonna say isn't sure who I am. At this point, question probably leans more to WHAT than who. Woman was out of her mind. Tried to turn a car key into me last I'd seen her. Still upstairs. For all I knew she was dead as well. Hadn't been up there in weeks. I mean, someone or something had to be dead in that place.

Funny enough (probably not funny but well . . .) one night Chris, very serious and straight-faced told me he thought SHE WAS DEAD! This, WHILE SHE WAS STANDING THERE TALKING TO US! I was like, wow, that's some strange and specific hereditary trait in this family. All thinking each other are dead.

Why I try and rationalize things I don't know. Guess it gives me something to do. I asked Chris, if your grandmother's dead how is it she's talking to us? He simply answered "she can do that." Which in all fairness WAS an answer.

I'd now officially spent half my life in Chris's basement watching him half nod and occasionally jump up and say "oh!" as if he forgot something. Yes. That was your life you'd forgotten there Chris. Me as well.

Over the years we did less and less. Never did much to start with so basically we did nothing.

Occasionally ordered Chinese food. Had a lengthy discussion once based on a fortune Chris received. Simply read: "What if the hokeypokey really is what it's all about?"

Yeah, pot is bad for the brain.

Our big outing took place once a month when we'd go to Chris's pot connection on Little West 12th Street in Manhattan. Connection sounds so glamorous. Our connection was a guy named Sam. Sam the Witch. We called him that because he belonged to some strange religion that believed wood was alive. Yes wood. I guess if you break it down, trees are alive so he did have a point but . . . well . . .

His pot was INTENSE! We called it Witch weed. Sam did not smoke. He drank. And drank. And drank. QUARTS of Vodka. "Once you get to the quarts it's just different," he'd occasionally mutter . . . and then cry . . . then mutter . . . and then sleep (faint).

We'd go to Sam's and spend the entire day. Had to. Last of a dying breed. Type who sells pot as a sort of communal thing. A service. Not about the money. About the experience. He enjoyed the social aspect of it. A nice thought in the right company. Not that this was the wrong company but, let's just say conversation was never a strong point amongst the players involved.

As the midday sun beat through his Tuesday-afternoon shades, the scene would play out.

Chris sitting in stifling silence as Sam the Witch would doze off mumbling in a low volume slowly rising. Higher and higher until he'd wake himself up, stand, apologize, and continue the cycle. Something like: "no . . . no . . . No . . . oh My God . . . Oh My GOD OH MY GOD NO!!!" He'd stand in a sweat.

"My God I'm sorry, so what were we talking about?" Sit back down and repeat.

Chris would pay no mind, busy smoking away. Once again I would sit and take note.

The Custodian Guy.

I used to watch the custodian guy in school. Back and forth with that mop. Back and forth. Who is he? Does he know that job sucks?

Sometimes I'd sit there for a long while after school. Of all people to put thoughts in your head, why would it be him?

Is he in love? Was he ever? Why was this custodian guy making me think all these thoughts? Weird.

At 18 you can attach things to yourself for money.

Enlightenment can come from the strangest of chances. A brush with death, a vision of God, and poof, everything changes. Some wake with the answer to an unimaginable mathematical problem. Some invent things. It's wide open. Mine came by way of an acne patch.

Back in high school you'd pass three storefronts on your way back to the subway home. An unemployment office, an Army recruiting station, and a human research laboratory.

One day a kid we knew, Oliver, came walking out scratching his back, holding a twenty and five singles, and bang. Nothing was ever the same.

Research lab was a place that would stick "tester patches" on consenting pupils' chests and backs for weeks at a time paying $25. That was it. Simple. Go live your life, come back in a week or two with or without a new rash, get your money.

The patches were usually new and untested brands of makeup or lotions that needed to prove they DIDN'T make human beings (us) break out in hives, acne, or whatever.

Whether you did or didn't break out you got your $25. But if you did, well, this was GREAT NEWS. In addition to your initial payment, all sorts of other things could now be tried on you to cure this breakout. These sometimes paid as much as $100. Once again proving the glass can be half full. Or, the rash half cured.

As you got older you became more capable of making legal and rational decisions about what should and should not be done to your body.

At twenty-one, "rational" would now be defined by "legal" as what "should and should not" be done **WITH** your body, would now be defined by what "could and could not" be done **TO** your body. And what "could" be done to you as an adult guinea pig can get pretty serious.

Once had a full conversation with a Pakistani man in hopes of selling both his corneas for $6,000 toward the dream of buying his own hack license for a cab. Thus, rendering him blind and unable to drive this cab. (Didn't wanna burst the dream as I simply agreed $6,000 was a lot of money.)

Basically people get nuts once the "anything goes" flag is raised.

As for me and Chris, we had found the answer to our dreams. At eighteen, while other teenagers dreamt of that twenty-first birthday when they could finally have that first legal drink at the bar, we'd been staring, licking our chops at the mere thought of all the things they could do and attach to us for money on that glorious day.

21.

The day we'd never have to do anything again.

After 21 they can attach things to you for more money.

What a life. And I mean that both sarcastic and joyously.

In the regular world me and Chris, well, didn't exist. Merely two quick rejections "sorry that job has been filled" in the long and monotonous day of some other lucky (unlucky) hiring schmuck's life. We were down to no more than three rejections a week (we'd go after three a week) and then return to the one place that would welcome us with open, well . . . things to attach to us.

We were now with the big boys of human product testing. An upgrade or downgrade depending on which way you looked at it. Never knew people could get so excited about an STD outbreak or cold sore. But here well, hey it meant straight-up cash.

I overheard a doctor at one of these things telling a colleague, "Yeah, curing cancer is one thing, but the guy who finds how to make that *dick* grow or put a little hair on someone's head . . . now that'll be a rich man!"

Seems, if the solution to one of those ailments was going to be found, one of us guinea pigs was gonna be the lucky recipient.

New York always seems to take everything to the extreme. Being a human lab experiment case study did not take exception.

Like with drug use, alcohol abuse, or anything questionable you must eventually evolve, devolve, advance, or digress. Basically stuff will get more crazy.

What started in acne patches moved on to nicotine patches, proceeded to hair-loss remedies (often resulting in a human mange look), and had now landed me and Chris into Mount Cyni for a one-week stint. (yes, I did notice it not only to be a play on Mount Sinai but also eerily close to cyanide).

Mount Cyni (real name) was a place appropriately located in Jamaica, Queens, where they ran lengthy tests on humans.

In the way slavery was abolished over two hundred years ago while people still work for minimum wage without health benefits, human experimenting still goes on and I'm here to tell you about it. Not complain, just tell.

Mine and Chris's human guinea pigging had landed us in Mount Cyni for one week to have adrenaline levels tested on us. Why adrenaline levels needed to be defined in humans was not for us to question. We were there to be tested ON.

They attached what's known as a gastric nasal adrenaline drip to us. A sort of morphine intravenous in reverse they had control of. We walked (often RAN) around the ward for a week wired out of our heads. But hey, did I mention it paid one thousand dollars apiece? This was the big time.

You'd sign a lengthy consent form they'd insist (sort of) you read. When I say "insist" think one long uninterested exhaled run-on sentence: "Make sure to read the consent form as we will not be liable for any and or all forms of maiming, health, or mental problems thank you." Gotta love consent forms that include the word "maiming."

We were so excited to legally be making $1,000 all I vaguely remember seeing on that form was some text mentioning the possibility that "veins could BURST in our EYES" or something. Wow! $1,000 though.

They had real calming (wait scratch that, NOTHING was calming about that place) well, the kind of music you heard in the movie, *One Flew Over the Cuckoo's Nest* was constantly pumped out from strategically placed areas at an almost undetectable volume. Undetectable to the normal ear. NOT the one ADRENALINE was being pumped into all week. (I took it as a personal mission to locate each and every one of those speakers.)

One afternoon I got into a game of Jenga with this big Russian guy (Brajko) being Chris slept almost the entire week. Strange reaction to adrenaline I thought, but Chris was always wired up all wrong.

Jenga turned into a near-violent death match between Brajko and some other MANIAC who called it a "fucking American Indian game!" And proceeded to smash the whole Jenga set against a wall.

Brajko replied in his strong and broken accent "hey I hate the fucking American Indian for as much as next guy but this is good fucking game!"

Far as I know, Jenga has nothing to do with American Indians but such is a day in the life at adrenaline testing.

Oscar Peterson

Where acne patches had led to adrenaline studies, an old black man (Oscar Peterson) now held the new key to the next phase of our lives.

Seemed adrenaline had the same drowsy effect on him as it did Chris. Unfortunately, same can't be said for the Indian hater who (no joke) BROKE the night window open and ran into the Jamaica, Queens, abyss never to be heard from again. Reminiscent of the Indian in *One Flew Over the Cuckoos Nest* (coincidence?).

So, on the drowsy front, Oscar Peterson who constantly dozing off pronounced his name *Oscuh Pe-ersoh*, slurred the city

Los *Angelllllles* to me. "Ya knooooow . . . in Los Angelllllllles they got these (I'm typing verrrrry slow in case you cannot tell) same t-hhhh(one long exhale on a hard *H*)hhhhypa gigs but safe and a whooooooole lot morrre . . . money." (In Los Angeles they have these same type of gigs but safe and they pay a lot more money.)

Between that, the $2,000 me and Chris made from adrenaline testing, and our teenage Bacardi-ad dreams of Los Angeles, we were there two weeks later.

Finally outta the black-light basement. Away from death. Ready for safer and higher-paying human research studies in the sun. Onward!

Last I remember Chris's Grandma, she was waving in the wrong direction from her front stoop. It was funny for a minute. Kind of. Walked over to give her a kiss on the cheek good-bye. Don't know why. We never had that or any kind of a relationship.

When I got close she whispered, "Now if I forget you next time I see you, don't you forget me OK?" Something real sad about that. Didn't know how to respond. Just something real sad about it.

She'll be fine I guess. The corpses are gone.

The long bus ride.

The entire experience of taking a bus cross country can best be explained by an occurrence me and Chris both witnessed while sidetracked with a flat tire near Flagstaff, Arizona. An elderly crack addict choked to death on her false teeth while two runaways fled into the midnight desert afraid they'd be accosted by the arriving police. No joke.

My escape is counting crows. All across America. Crows are everywhere. Chris sleeps while I count them. Drifting off. My mind focuses once again on that custodian guy. The one from grade school.

What am I gonna do with my life has become a statement I simply mutter to myself. Who would love me can be a terrifying question to ask yourself.

Being alone, worst of all. Chris fills that void in the strangest of ways. Not entirely. Actually sometimes not at all. But somehow his company. Us together isn't as bad as me alone.

Los Angeles. The corpses have arrived.

If you move to Pittsburgh you'll probably find yourself talking about steel mines a lot. Same if you were Puppet or Mike Murphy in Queens.

On Wall Street you most likely saw tech stocks on the rise before the common man did.

In Los Angeles you talk about entertainment. It's the steel mine of this city. Takes getting used to. At first I'd be like, "Why can't that guy just say he's an electrician? Why does he have to be an electrician on *FRASIER*?"

You eventually realize that EVERYONE here in one way or another ends up in the entertainment industry. If you're a plumber you just might find yourself being the plumber for the set of *The O.C.* They have toilets, too.

Just seems weird. Fixing a broken sink for Tony Danza just sounds so much better than plumbing at the OTB on Northern Blvd.

East Coast and West Coast have funny trade-offs. Frankfurters for corn dogs, pizza for tacos, and, well, acne patches for what's known as marketing research.

Music to my ears. Marketing research. No more attachments, intravenous, diet pills, or long terribly scary consent forms.

Marketing research was the dream inside the dream. The prize inside the Cracker Jacks.

Maryanne can hook you up in the world of marketing research.

Upon arrival in Los Angeles Chris gave up pot. Spur of the moment. Cold turkey. No withdrawals or particular reason. Poof, it was over. We were on to a new chapter.

We met a woman named Maryanne. Once you got on her list she'd call practically every day sending you on endless marketing research gigs.

Typical phone call from her would be short and to the point. No messing around. Always admired how she'd bypass (completely) the normal greetings and get directly to the fact of the matter.

"6 PM tonight, 10267 Ventura Boulevard. tell them you have a small family, own a Dodge Durango. You're always interested in the latest models coming out. Pays $50." (Hang up)

"4:15 104 Hauser Avenue, you and your entire family enjoy alcoholic beverages. Especially sangrias. You've been married seven years. Pays $55." (Hang up)

My favorites were the computer-related ones. Maryanne was from a different era, computers were way too futuristic for her taste. Last generation of scheisters. Schemers. Snake-oil salespeople.

Computers always threw her for a loop. "11 AM 222 North Vermont you have to have windows on your . . . or a window computer or . . . you own computers and have windows or something in your house. Pays $85." (Hang up)

Her calls were always in a sort of code. As if you were on some kind of spy mission. For a laugh we'd sometimes try and get either a hello or good-bye out of her being she was not there to chitchat, simply the facts. I'd attempt an "OK thanks Maryanne, you take care."

Once actually got a pause and then a " . . . yeah" before she hung up, which I considered a victory. You claim what you can.

Marketing research is done through test groups. Companies hire someone (Maryanne) to hire twenty to thirty "target consumers" to see what they like and don't like about a particular product they are familiar with.

With this information they figure how to advertise and make whatever product they're researching more appealing to that specific demographic. Unfortunately, we (the hired "target consumers") are seldom part of the demographic they're looking for.

Maryanne gets a kickback for each person she gets to show up. An agent of sorts. Soon as she knows what they're looking for, she'll call and tell us who or what to pretend to be. Low-end beer or sodas are easy as we ARE that demographic. Lexus-driving family man with a six-figure income, particularly interested in aeronautics, a different story. One she'll make up for us.

As all things in Los Angeles do lead to entertainment, we'd sometimes get gigs for movies.

For $50 they'd want our opinions on which poster they should run on buses for a particular film. Which one would make you (target consumer) wanna go out and spend the twelve bucks?

We were called in for one starring Billy Crystal and Robin Williams. They were targeting families looking for a night out. We came as concerned PTA parents who enjoyed "family nights out." Showed us three different posters they were thinking of running. Just went ahead and picked one. Said it made me feel like we'd all really enjoy it (yeah, all of us). "Especially the young ones."

Chris, most days, is usually quite lethargic to say the least. Out of absolutely nowhere, he LOUDLY contributed, "Well that one over there repulses me!" (It was one with Robin Williams riding piggyback on Billy Crystal.)

Thought I was hearing things. Before I could even look up he was on to the second poster. "And that one makes me think all kinds of violence might be about to erupt!" (Billy Crystal and Robin Williams in "gang attire" spray painting a wall.) "And that one's just plain dumb." (Billy Crystal doing a sort of "oh no" Macaulay Culkin gesture while Robin Williams closes his eyes.)

I almost burst out in laughter. It was so completely out of character I was sure I was hearing things.

They told him these were the only three posters to choose from. Chris responded that he'd rather be *DEAD* then go see it if those were his only options.

The research and advertising people seemed nervous and paid us to basically leave. I was speechless. Don't recall ever laughing so hard in my life. Getting paid to leave was a whole avenue of unexplored terrain.

Fact that Chris found NO humor in it made it all the more funnier. What a strange afternoon that was. He still periodically brings up how appalled he was by those posters. I chalked, and chalk it up to the only known withdrawal symptoms from his giving up pot.

This did open me to the idea that the people running these research gigs could care less as well.

At first I'd get worried seeing the same interviewers at different gigs. On Monday I'd be telling one I was a single man who had just lost three pounds through a certain diet pill. Wednesday I'd be explaining which airline I preferred flying with my family of five to the same guy.

Eventually I realized all they wanted was to jot down my lies, pay me my $45, collect theirs, and go home. This took all the fear out of it. Even got to know one of the research guys (Ricky). He'd half smile as I'd go from father of four to dental technician to wine connoisseur to motorcycle enthusiast sometimes in a mere two days.

Once in a while you do run into someone who takes this job seriously. These kinds always drove me crazy. Reminded me of the guy you work side by side with at a fast food place that rats you out for eating a fry or something.

When you come across them, double-talk becomes your best friend. We had buzzwords or phrases when cornered.

If it had to do with computers and you felt trapped, one phrase Maryanne was big on telling them was "the market is expanding for software." That was it. She'd heard someone say it on some computer show she was watching, and it became our panic button (ejector seat).

Say for instance you came up against a skeptical interviewer who actually gave a damn. Their question being, "Do you prefer to use a Mac or PC for transferring personal data for business?" Well, "The market is expanding for software."

See, the people running these research gigs are in the same financial hell you are, trust me. Reminds me of people embarrassed to ask a guy working at a bank for a loan. What do you think, that guy's got so much money he decided to be a teller?

Well if your computer researcher was a stickler, just drop the old "market is expanding for software" which would often make him or her feel like you actually knew something they didn't. Before they were found out to not be knowledgeable enough to be conducting computer surveys, they'd likely pay and send you on your way.

The market expanding for software can vary.

We got a call one day from Maryanne about a gig paying $700 for two hours of work. You mean WITHOUT intravenous being involved?

Had to pretend to be anesthesiologists. Maryanne knew we owned two pairs of scrubs and well, I guess that qualified us enough to get the gig.

Thought, *Who's gonna be nuts enough to believe we're anesthesiologists?* Maryanne's reasoning was no one was gonna believe anyone would be nuts enough to PRETEND they were anesthesiologists.

Maryanne was like Charlie from *Charlie's Angels*. No one ever saw her. She'd call in with missions, not entirely unlike those from the show. Send us on some yet unforeseen mission involving false identities, costumes, and, well, you can understand the comparison.

We each had pictures in our mind as to what she looked like. I pictured a kind of short wacky college-y professor. Hector and Rodriguez, two Mexican guys who also did these research gigs thought she was probably hot (nothing I can imagine would lead ANYONE to this conclusion). Chris didn't speculate.

She'd call with an address, your mission, who you had to be, your pay, and always a few troubleshooting remedies in case you found yourself in a tough spot.

"If they ask what dosages of some knockout drug you apply when doing your operations just keep saying, *it varies.*" What varies? She'd say, "The hell do I know, just keep saying *it varies* about whatever they ask when you have no idea what they're talking about." This was the medical version of "the market is expanding for software."

Maryanne's living came from making sure these research gigs had enough willing participants at them. She, like the rest of us and them, could care less about the outcomes. Funny. An entire business built around research and information that everyone involved in is lying.

At the anesthesiologist research lab (crappy abandoned office space in the Valley) we ran into Hector and Rodriguez. Or should I say, Dr. Hector and his trusted associate Rodriguez. We exchanged (very doctorly) greetings and walked on with our scams. "Dr. Martinez."

Half an hour and $700 later we met for bean and cheese burritos at Baja Fresh down the block.

MARTINEZ (*laughs, chowing down burrito*)
Yes. I tell her in my country sometimes we have to weigh the medications, so the dosages it varies. And then she say which kinds I use and I say it varies again. (*laughs*)

I imagine it's all pretty immoral. Lying for a living. Impersonating. But, well, everyone knew. Just making a buck ya know? Having a little fun here and there.

The anesthesiologist one was a bit nerve-racking for me. Got a little reckless. Instead of the old "it varies," I went off course.

You get bored ya know? Boredom can breed carelessness. I got careless. Tried to actually name a dosage amount of some drug I had no idea what it was.

Said I preferred admitting 10,000 cc's of it as opposed to the normal 5,000 cc recommendation when putting "my" patients under. Seems whoever I was overruling with that call was only trying to KILL a small VILLAGE. I must have been going for a city! (appropriate amount was 5 cc's, not 5,000! I read it wrong.) They corrected me, I laughed, "But of course."

For every survey there was a back door, every curve they threw, an angle. One they barely ever questioned you entering through. Long as you were presentable enough for them to put your name on paper everything was fine. Everyone got paid.

A mere confusing statement could get you out of even the tightest of situations.

Success rate of getting paid was comparable to the rate of noninformation these surveys were obtaining. Near 100 percent.

In all our times of doing these marketing research gigs, I can only remember one time leaving empty-handed. A $500 gig for pilots. Airplane pilots. Chris and I got cornered in some serious aeronautics talk and the ol' "yeah 747s just aren't the best bird in the sky anymore" just wasn't cutting it that day.

No one bats a thousand.

If You Ask Me Honestly

I'll answer you the same way. I live a terrified existence. In fear. Fear of abandonment, failure, success (not yet a problem). I'm basically a scaredy-cat. It's awful to be this way but the truth. Sucked my thumb til I was . . . still do in secret. Read that it was some sort of abandonment-issue type thing and I'm pretty sure it is.

Had a mother and father that would pass every lie detector you could strap to them asking if they were the best parent they could possibly be.

They wouldn't be lying because they were. Just happened to not be good enough it seems. They say only a child lucky enough to have been given love can find a way to question that love. I guess I'm lucky that way. I was blanketed with love and found fifty ways to condemn it. That's OK. I am what I am for now.

Consumer Psychological Home Reports

With all the different ways of getting paid in the Los Angeles research world I've wondered how anyone ever ends up broke. I mean, me and Chris certainly don't have a yacht or anything but we're fine. We eat out all the time at Astro Burger, have our own apartments, stocked refrigerators, a little extra to see a movie now and then. Life is about as good as it gets. Who needs a yacht anyway? Who *has* a yacht?

Every day brings a new adventure, a new cola to test, new vacuum to compare, a new . . . who knows? I remember comparing different soils once. Dirts! Believe I was supposed to be an agriculturist or something. Nuts. "Yeah, this one is obviously more moist." Yeah.

By far the best research gigs were the ones you'd do from home. "Consumer Psychological Home Reports." You'd get them in the mail, usually along with a disposable camera. They'd ask you to take photographs based on their instructions.

We did one for this Alzheimer's place. Requirement was that you lived with a family member who had the disease. Well, we actually did live with Chris's grandmother . . . just not at this time. You find ways to justify things. Funny how that goes.

They sent us a camera and asked we take the appropriate photos in conjunction with their numbered assignments. I'll break it down.

1. With your first photo please take a picture of a place
   you enjoy taking your family member with Alzheimer's
   for an outing.

Went to the nearest coffee shop, held the door for an old lady as Chris took a photo of me and her smiling. (There's me and Grandma at her favorite restaurant.)

2. With your second photo please take a picture of your
   ailing loved one in their favorite part of the house.

Being we couldn't talk that same old lady into coming to Sears with us, we went and wandered around the Home and Appliance section there and took a photo of another old lady standing near a stove. Yeah, Aunt Rose has Alzheimer's, too.

What these surveys were attempting to find out were things like, what would make their ads most appealing to families looking to stick poor ol' Grandma in a nursing home. We were simply trying to make twenty-five bucks.

Years would go by. As we closed in on thirty it was hard to not even begin to consider the term "loser," but life was good.

Perfectly content in the world (racket) of marketing research, I'd of spent the rest of my life in it. Could of gone happily to my grave testing and retesting the more satisfying taste of Miller vs Bud, Whopper vs the Quarter Pounder, the durability of sandwich bags.

A different plan was in the works.

Audience Participation Placement

One night after giving all we had as far as connoisseurs in the field of various gums (Trident vs Wrigley's) we ran into one of our fellow market researchers, Hector, on a bus.

Couldn't join us at Astro Burger being he had to get up early for a taping of a TV show called *Judge Abrahms*. Didn't say it like that. Said he was coming home from an audience participation placement job. Mistakenly said "perspiration" but I knew what he meant.

Went on to explain how you can get paid $50 to sit in the audience of horrible television shows. Shows so bad they can't even get tourists to show up to. The $50 is to sit, fill seats, and do whatever the prompter tells you. Laugh, clap, "oooh," hiss, yell, anything. "Even give you coffee and doughnuts and sometimes lunch."

Says there's gigs every day. "Ask Maryanne about them."

Even Chris looked interested. He wasn't. Just looked like it.

And this is where my story begins. The one worth telling.

The Clapper

All night this new term, "audience participation placement,"
was on my mind. What was it? How could I have not heard about
it? Thought I knew all the rackets in this world.

Next morning I asked Maryanne. Without hesitation she went
right into it.

Basically a CLAPPER is a paid audience member set up to make
people believe human beings are actually attending (enthusiastically)
HORRIBLE TV shows no one has ever heard of. Basically, they do
have LAUGH TRACKS to fool the audience at home, but every once
in a while they like to flash the camera at an audience actually doing
it for real. Clapping, laughing, etc. Thinking behind it is well,
"They're enjoying it so it must be good." It isn't. Ever. Hardly.

Maryanne would enthusiastically call. "I have two shows on Monday paying $50 each, an infomercial paying a hundred on Tuesday, and another on Thursday where they want to shoot someone out of a cannon."

Excited she had an in with this scene, I was still taken back a bit by the "cannon" statement. Always admired how she never even flinched at the absurdity of ANY request. So utterly jaded and used to the absurd I couldn't imagine anything ever fazing her.

Remember her once sending me on a research job where in her words "pays $35, they want to **burn someone alive.**" I said WHAT? She hesitated, "Oh, I meant, pays $35 where they wanna *turn someone's life* around. Not burn someone alive." No laugh. No nothing. Just a correction.

I imagine if that request were real she'd of found a taker. Next day when she didn't hear back because well, that taker was BURNT ALIVE, she'd just move on to the next name on the list.

Not that Maryanne wasn't a good person. Just doing her job.

I asked what the requirements for doing these shows were. "Just show up alive and do whatever the prompter tells you to."

Asked what the cannon deal was about. "Some kind of skit where they pick an audience member and pretend to shoot you out of a cannon or something. Pays $200." "Do they really shoot you out of a cannon? Is it dangerous?" I asked. She responded, half listening, by once again repeating, "Yeah, it pays $200."

From here on I'd found my calling. Long gone were the days of acne patches and dangerous consent forms. Gone too the days of Coke vs Pepsi marketing research. The entertainment bug had found and bitten me. Me and Chris. We were headed to television. The audience of television. The paid audience of television.

Occasionally we'd still do some marketing research gigs but more and more it was audience participation placement. We called it Clapping. They called us Clappers. I was a Clapper.

There certainly was something strange about enjoying a job. Something almost guilty about it. Looking forward to going to work seemed unnatural.

See, even though the shows were terrible, you eventually got to know most of the Clappers. Pay was OK. They'd even feed you sometimes. Work was pretty consistent and after all, we were in show business. A form of it at least. Everyone in the city was.

How to make money.

Fun isn't everything ya know? My mother used to say that.

With our new adventures in the entertainment industry we had to figure a way to actually earn a living on a consistent basis. Working day to day can be mentally exhausting. Just waiting for that call so you can come in, clap, and chip away at that phone bill, rent, or get some food can really wear you down.

After digging around we figured if you were a straight-up Clapper you could earn anywhere from $50 to $75 a show. On a good day you could do as many as three.

Job was simple. Sit in a chair, watch the teleprompters and do what they say. Laugh, applaud, hiss.

At the end of each show (about two hours), you'd get on what most resembled a warped Communion/AA line and receive your check. Think monkey (us) hitting light (clapping) when light turns green (teleprompter) banana (check) falls out.

Funny to actually use that banana analogy being sometimes when they felt us Clappers weren't lively enough they'd call a break in the filming, bring out some HORRENDOUS comedian/cheerleader who'd blow whistles and throw chocolate to (at) us. This was to get us "in the laughing mood" I guess.

The bigger pay was in the audience PARTICIPATION aspect of the gig. This meant you got to talk or be a "volunteer."

Nothing in the world of bad TV and infomercials is spontaneous. Nothing. That woman randomly chosen from the audience to taste that spaghetti sauce they just made: a paid professional. That enthusiastic "*mmmm*" she lets out: scripted. Lady probably flirted with some low-end infomercial producer for that gig. The gig of a lifetime. Her big break. Pretend to like the spaghetti sauce, get paid.

To be an actual participant in these infomercials paid you extra and gave you something to do. Chris was once picked to jump up and down on an "unbreakable plate" and ask astonished, "Why doesn't this dish break?" Earned him an extra $100 in addition to the $50 for simply sitting in the audience. That's called a "speaking volunteer." A doubly good deal. Bad casting but a doubly good deal.

To avoid this extra pay they'd usually ask that you express this "astonishment" silently. Thus making you a "non-speaking volunteer." A $50 bonus as opposed to $100.

The whole scene can basically make you nuts. Eventually you don't want to do anything for free. Laugh, clap, nothing. After a while, every time you crack a smile you expect a few bucks from somebody. You get crazy. So full of value you just don't know what to do with yourself.

We'd look upon tourists, lining up by the dozens for major network sitcoms, like people being handed brooms and voluntarily sweeping the streets. Called them "Clappers Gone Wild." Suckers.

Luckily for us our shows were so unwatchable they literally had to pay people to walk through their doors. The doors we walked in.

The order of succession.

I don't want to mislead you. I loved this job. Both me and Chris. Putting things in perspective though, our previous ones did come with warnings including the possibility of temporary and/or permanent blindness. Case in point, a beautiful pig is still a pig.

Being a Clapper is certainly the bottom of the entertainment food chain. Most of us recognize that, others consider it a mere stutter, or bump on the road to success. The latter being "crazy" people, aka Clappers With Agendas (CWA).

Basically most Clappers With Agendas aspire to be extras who aspire to be "speaking" extras who aspire to be walk-on guests who aspire to be recurring characters who . . . get what I mean? Crazy.

Hey, AC/DC said, "It's a long way to the top if you wanna rock 'n' roll."

Being at the bottom of any food chain, though, certainly doesn't mean you unequivocally must aspire to move up from it. Oceans bottom's probably full of paramecium perfectly fine being hunted by shrimp.

On the flipside, being at the bottom doesn't mean you necessarily have to recognize that's where you're at, either. A whole slew of Clappers were merely "earning a little extra cash while I'm . . . " or "doing research for . . . " These particular stars and starlets of the clapping and infomercial world no longer "aspired" . . . but had long ago arrived. Risen. Accomplished in their own rights. (out of their minds) "Emperors with no clothes" of sorts.

By the coffee machine you'd often overhear boasts of, "I've had speaking roles on upwards of 157 infomercials." Claims of, "I have no interest in moving on to film." Delusions of Grandeur.

Don't let this overheard sense of accomplishment at the water cooler fool you though. Toss a bone in this crowd and there'd be a bloodfest.

Early in my days in the circuit (almost said circus) I was on the set of some infomercial when that guy with the question marks all over his suit showed up. I'm sure you've seen him on at least half a dozen of them. A considerable "star" in this world. Let's not forget what world we're talking about though. Upon his arrival you'd of thought Clark Gable'd graced the palace.

Clappers crowded around. Pope had arrived! Hoping for a

nod. Any scrap of acknowledgment. "Did your show two years ago about the water filters!" Question Mark Guy just walked on through. Couldn't be bothered. One adoring fan apologized on his behalf, "He gets that all the time."

Geronimo likes to ask questions.

Amongst the accomplished "infomercialites" was our friend Geronimo.

Not "Mr." Geronimo or Geronimo "something." Simply Geronimo. Said he was Native American but looked much more Indian, as in from India, to me.

Geronimo took any chance he got to shine as literally just that. His chance to shine. I must preface this with the fact that he was not "looking" for his big break, that had come long ago. Geronimo had no aspirations of being discovered. He was already a star ten times over. This had taken place years ago in his mind.

You've heard the analogy of wanting to be the big fish in a small pond. Geronimo was perfectly content being the tadpole in the fish tank. The sperm in the test tube. Infomercial audiences were not the stepping-stone but the plateau.

Stopped at Kinko's every morning to print out yet another twenty black-and-white headshots (from 20 years ago) along with his résumé (12 pages stapled together). These were much more about letting you know who he was rather than actually drumming up any further work. A reminder of the magnitude of the person you were dealing with.

If a camera had so much as panned by him in the audience of an episode of the *Mike Douglas Show* in 1987 it was on there.

"Featured Moment on *Mike Douglas Show* June 15th 1987."

Must had given me 20 copies over the years to give to "people" for him.

Geronimo loved to PARTICIPATE in the shows. Nothing to do with the extra money earned, he was simply looking for a chance to perform. Lengthen his résumé.

Whole point of a paid audience was to blend in. To NOT look like it was the same people in the audiences of all the shows. They wanted the viewing audience (from home) to believe people were lining up by the dozens, flocking to fill seats. Dying to hear about this new "miracle car wax."

Because Geronimo was an EYEsore he was seldom chosen to ask or participate on any of the shows. Think, the Indian crying on that old TV commercial meets Ghandi meets I don't know what.

Besides his striking appearance, Geronimo liked to enhance, or make the most of, his time on camera.

See, if you were picked to participate (ask a question) on an infomercial they would approach you about half an hour before filming started. Hand you a line and that was it.

Geronimo would take this note and immediately turn the bathroom (Porto-Potty) into his private dressing/rehearsal room.

He'd emerge a few minutes before filming, refreshed, well rehearsed, with a full rewrite. Nuts.

Give him a few lines like "I have a question, I like to eat hamburgers at night and with these new miracle pills will I still lose weight?" Simple.

His well-rehearsed and Shakespeareanly performed rewrite would magically become "I have a question for you that I believe can be answered. In my evenings I sometimes enjoy a good hamburger, sometimes two, not to mention the accompaniment of a good-sized portion of french fries (contrived laugh). If I continue to do so while adding your new miracle pills to my palate will I still lose weight?"

We all loved Geronimo for this. "No small part, small actor." He'd say with the phoniest Indian accent ever (straight outta old cowboy movies). Geronimo was the best. He'd fight endlessly with producers about how his lines were better than theirs and eventually give in, never entirely, though.

Always sneak in at least one of his rewritten lines for some sort of personal affirmation. I recall "palate" once.

Louise makes sure you watch the prompters and don't fall asleep.

Certainly was strange enjoying going to work. Even looked forward to it at times.

Practically no way you could screw the gig up. Show up on time, stay below the radar, and don't fall asleep. Pretty much the only rules other than don't show up naked with a gun.

If there was one challenge it would be staying awake. Listening to them filming the same unfunny jokes over and over made even laughing an art. Eventually mastering it by finding ways to do it with your eyes closed (wear dark sunglasses).

When you stick around long enough, you start to realize or accept that maybe bad jokes are better than good ones, when repeated over and over.

Watched a guy slip on a dishrag twenty-five times once. First five weren't funny at all.

Last twenty I was laughing so hard they actually asked me to tone it down.

Clappers are considered "behind the scenes." The offscreen laughter behind a joke, the "booing" when the villain arrives, the faces quickly panned by to let you (at home) know you're not the only one watching this crap.

Behind the scenes of behind the scenes is Louise. If Maryanne the producer is the Charlie from *Charlie's Angels*, Louise would be Bosley. I guess that would leave me, Chris, and Geronimo as the Angels.

Louise is the Maryanne you actually get to see. Another producer. The on-location one. Maryanne sends you, Louise greets you (sort of).

She'll meet you (us Clappers) at the gate and send you to various locations in the studios. Different lots, stages. "*Judge Abrahms* at Lot 1 needs three enthusiastic Clappers." "Lot 14 needs eleven standard audience members." "Lot 7 has an infomercial paying a bonus $150 for someone who doesn't mind eating something hot onstage . . . VERY hot."

Aside from delegating, Louise has three jobs. Stop us from sleeping on camera, make sure you react appropriately to the prompter (don't BOO when it says LAUGH), and hand out the bananas (payment) after the show.

Louise looked like Rhoda. In case you didn't know, anyone can be described as either looking like or a combination of strange washed-up '70s and '80s TV sitcom characters. Try it. You'll see.

Well Louise looked like Rhoda. Actually Rhoda mixed with Janet from *Three's Company*. Joyce Dewitt. Her job was to make sure we followed the prompters and basically stayed below the radar (no LOUD shirts).

Another no-nonsense producer. Louise never minded that NONE of us EVER watched any of the shows. Long as we did our job, all was fine. We'd sit eating sandwiches from home in paper bags quietly conversing while doing whatever the prompter told us to. To get a better visual of it try this:

Imagine some awful infomercial filming in a studio. Think *Alf* with a REAL cheap puppet, NOT funny, selling retractable head screwdrivers. You're sitting in the audience as a Clapper, amongst Clappers. While the show's filming, you quietly break out your paper-bag lunch. Baloney sandwich or something.

Actors are straight ahead but the prompter giving you instructions as to how to react (to what you're not watching) is to the left. As you eat your sandwich you ONLY watch the prompter as opposed to the show while quietly conversing with your friend Chris about say, the weather. "Yeah I hear it's supposed to rain I think on Saturday and (LOUD LAUGHTER SIGN BLINKS) HAHAHAHAHAHAHAHAHAH! (Then back to conversation) "Yeah, well I was hoping for a sunny day ya know, go to the beach or something."

In between takes you can sit for hours. We had all kinds of things to keep us busy. Play dumb games. "Name the most embarrassing place you could be caught alone in by friends." Our friend Geronimo hands down won this with his choice. Sitting alone at Benihana in front of the chef doing his big display for you and you only. Funny.

Usually the shows were horrible but sometimes mildly enter-taining. Even the infomercials could get you sometimes. Went and bought a "sporkiplate" once with all the money I made sitting in the audience of that very same infomercial. Seemed like a great idea. Actually was a great idea but did I really need a spoon/fork/knife and plate all in one? Still own it. So useful it's actually useless.

All in all it was pretty fun just being around TV show sets. Even if they were horrible. Money was good and life was, too.

The art of staying invisible.

As mentioned, standing out in the crowd was the last thing you'd wanna do in this business. Being chosen to ask a question can be a blessing and a curse. You got your hundred dollars but God forbid that was the day you wore your new favorite Hawaiian shirt.

One standout moment and you could be off Louise and Maryanne's calling list for a month.

We all have our war stories, near fatal mishaps. Had a beard fall off while sleeping on a taping of *Judge Abrahms* once. Luckily Chris picked it up, nervously stuck it back on, no one noticed.

Forgettable attire, a normal haircut, no visible bruising or black eyes and you were fine.

Add an accessory every month or two (for a change), you were good as new.

Between shows we'd sometimes switch clothes, exchange fake beards, trade sunglasses, all kinds of hats. It can get pretty fun out in the waiting area. Think *Let's Make a Deal* but FOR REAL.

There are always rumblings of dissatisfaction but such is life. Geronimo wanted to start a union for a minute but couldn't find anything that rhymed with "clapping" to make a legitimate slogan.

Got us all amped on the idea doing his best Native American Hoffa impersonation. Reminding us from atop a water cooler that when you watch those old sitcoms like the *Odd Couple* or *The Dick Van Dyke Show.* "Those Clappers from then, ones laughing in audience, they all dead now!" "That all dead people laughing on them." "Dead people no residual!"

Union talks came and went but ever since that speech, the thought of watching any of those old shows accompanied by fifty or sixty dead people laughing still straight-up creeps me out.

Life was good. Saved up a little money and bought myself a Honda hatchback. First car I ever owned. Lime green. Horrible color. Cheapest one on the lot though. But why make one that color? It's as if the maker was like, "You want it cheap? Not without allowing us to humilliate you then."

Laura Ingalls.

In high school, for a minute I had a girlfriend. Laura Ingalls. Yup, like the show. Except this one smoked dust. A lot. Our understanding was, well, more like her demands were, under no circumstances (torture included) was I to EVER admit to anyone we dated. Never understood why she was with me but was always afraid she'd dump me if I asked. After a year of our secret relationship, on a bad trip, she thought I was the devil and jumped off a roof to her death. That was the one and only relationship in my life. Laura Ingalls. It wasn't hard to get over, more confusing. All my life I secretly thought about love though. Who doesn't? Not just the dust-free kind where you can hold hands in public. Kind that makes you whole. Fills you. Makes everything all worth it.

Judy.

At night, sometimes every night, sometimes every other, I'd go and get gas at a station on Santa Monica Boulevard by Gower. Right over by where we'd do our shows.

Two to three dollars a night from Judy. She's the attendant there. Works the night shift. Just enough gas to keep me coming back on a consistent basis.

All the guys from the shows have a thing for her. Looks like, well she hates when I say this but a real pretty version of Vera from the old TV show *Alice*. If Vera kept her hair like Olive Oyl (in that sort of bun thing) but real pretty.

After work (Clapping) the guys will sometimes joke, "Looks like time to get some gas huh?" I don't joke with them. I'm not uptight but Judy isn't a joke to me.

First time I saw her I was on line waiting to get some gas. Nothing too eventful. Guy in front of me was giving her a hard time. Real jerk. She seemed more shaken than mad. Jerk goes and slips on a banana peel. Really! A banana peel. What are the odds? Think I'd been waiting to see that ever since Saturday morning cartoons.

Guy jumped up nonchalantly, looked around, rustled back into his jalopy and sped away. I cracked up. Looked over at Judy. She looked down and away smiling. Then burst into laughter somewhat apologetically. Wouldn't make eye contact. Patch on her shirt said Judy. Everything from then on was different. Hi Judy.

Slowly she began warming up to me. I'd joke with her about just bad jokes ya know? Like, I don't know . . . so when's the parole hearing? Being she was always in that box.

One day she figured out why I only got $2 of gas a night. "You like coming to see me don't you?" I didn't come back for three nights. Came back and straight-faced tried ordering $5 being I was "gonna be gone a few days." We both couldn't help but crack a smile and from then on Judy's gas station became my nightly hangout.

I bought a beach chair from a Save-On drugstore. Foldable kind. Stuck it in the back of my car. Pulled it out every night and sat right there by her box. Sometimes the whole shift (10 pm to 6 am). We'd just talk all night back and forth through her loudspeaker.

Night shift, doors were always locked and she wasn't allowed outside til her shift was done. Fine with me, long as we could talk.

We'd joke that sometimes it was like she was on the moon cuz I'd be just sitting there on this beach chair looking up with her voice coming from the speaker placed high up by the gas pump. Funny.

Judy's everything. Everything you could ever want in a person. She's nice, funny. Actually hysterical. We'd play these ridiculous games together being there aren't many customers at night. Comparing them to TV sitcom people when they would show up. Try and make our own shows with them.

One lady looked EXACTLY like Mrs. Roper from the TV show *Three's Company*. EXACTLY. She'd come in with those awful perms and expensive gowns that look more like colorful pajamas. We had her paired up with a sort of overgrown Gary Coleman that used to come in nightly and order (with a serious tic) "Parliament (click) I said Par . . . (click) I said a pack a Parliament OK?"

There was another guy with a big old broken-down Cadillac who looked just like Benson from that awful show. We stuck the three of them on some new spy show hunting down washed-up sitcom actors.

On occasion someone would roll in that kinda looked like . . . OH IT IS Burt Reynolds! This was Hollywood after all.

We'd sit out all night just talking and laughing. I'd tell her my ideas, big plans, she'd tell me her dreams (always wanted to manage a pet store). She'd play me cassettes of songs she'd record off the radio. Play them over the loudspeaker.

Our favorite was Brian Wilson's "Love and Mercy." Especially the opening when he says "I was sitting in a crumby movie with my hand on my chin." We both agreed "crumby" was a great word. Underused.

Finding Judy was like meeting that kid in grade school you just clicked with. Whole world went away. Hours could pass on that beach chair looking up at that moon. Talking away. When that would happen, I'd lean over, take a peek. There she was. Judy. You wish these things could go on forever.

I know she almost got married once but the guy left her. Stole a bunch of her money, left her car impounded. The kinda girl you'd be saving up to get her car out of impoundment for! I like her a lot but I'm just awful at asking people on dates. I'd hate to make things uncomfortable in any way between us.

Geronimo tells me I should save up and take her somewhere nice. Somewhere with wine or something. Says there'd be no reason to ask her out til I saved up some money. "She can be broke on own." "Don't need you for that!"

With the Clapping gigs going well and some marketing research on the side, I planned to have enough for a wine date with Judy in no time.

Any old Tuesday

I come home one Tuesday from sitting out with Judy around 11:30. Early night. Jay Leno's on the TV. I like coming home to the TV on. Makes you feel like someone's there. I sit, as always after coming back from Judy, staring more through it than at it. She's in all my thoughts. Way she's gotten comfortable enough to say, through the speakers, "Oh Eddie, don't ya just love when everyone goes to sleep?" Just makes you wanna melt right into your sofa.

Jay Leno's doing one of his skits showing an infomercial I was actually at. Catches my attention. An AWFUL one. Awful's a tough word to use here because in this world awful can sometimes be a compliment. I mean, a good infomercial is awful right? So sometimes an awful one can, well, you get it. The world here is upside down my friend, and mine was about to go right along with it.

I was drinking from a container of juice because I'm always drinking from a container of juice. Wow, that was a great sentence huh?

The infomercial was trying to push costumes for dogs. Halloween, Christmas, sweaters, booties, the whole deal. Everybody needs that stuff right? I remembered this one in particular because we were stuck in the filming of it for about three hours. One of the dogs attacked the trainer trying to stick a captain's hat on its head.

So Jay Leno's showing this part where they're talking about how much the dogs "love these things." A standard poodle is quite uncomfortably wearing a cape, top hat, and Dracula teeth that keep falling out of its mouth. The host of the infomercial keeps putting them back in trying to act nonchalant about it. "Best part is the teeth are actually MEAT FLAVORED, so the dogs'll keep them in for hours!" A PETA nightmare.

They cut back to Jay doing a monologue on how awful some of these shows are. "I mean, WHO buys these things?"

Slowly his routine goes from *who* sits at **home** watching these things to *who* sits in the **audiences** watching these things!

"Hard as you all may find these things to watch on TV from the comfort of your living rooms, we seem to have found someone that well . . . seeks them out. Here take a look." Camera swings over to . . .

This is that moment.

Your life can change on a dime. A moment. A flash. I've heard horror stories. Strokes of luck. Apple lands on Newton's head, guy goes down a genius. Safe lands on some poor schmuck, he's an eternal punch line. The comedian Dennis Leary had a joke. Something about how he'd never live in New York. Too many tall buildings. Said you could find the cure for cancer, one day someone throws a cat off a roof, lands on your head and kills you. For eternity you're the "Cat Guy." Fate certainly is an uncertain venture.

So I'm watching and somewhat enjoying the Jay Leno show, recapping my night with Judy when he says that line: "Hard as you all may find these things to watch on your television sets, we seem to have found someone that well . . . seeks them out. Here take a look."

My recollection from here on is hazy. Vaguely recall the camera swinging over to ME asking a question from an ABERS-CIZER infomercial.

"I would like to lose weight but just hate to give up doughnuts."

Yup. That was it. They wrote it, I said it, and from here on my life would never be the same. This was that moment for me. Whether this would turn to be Newton's apple or a safe had yet to be determined.

The magic of television.

I was now officially asking millions of viewers on the Jay
Leno show if I really had to give up doughnuts. As his audience
laughed, the paid Clappers from the infomercial sat "intrigued"
(an actual teleprompter direction). The experience was somewhat three-dimensional. Entirely three-dimensional. I stood
there frozen in my living room holding my juice container.

All I could visualize as they continued laughing was that
infomercial's teleprompter blinking "INTRIGUED."

As if Jay Leno's editor knew exactly what I was thinking, the
show began quickly cutting back and forth between this frozen
image they have of me asking that question, to the paid infomercial audience's look of "intrigue."

JAY LENO

. . . and then my producers and I . . . as we're scanning
through tapes of all these shows are like wait a minute.
Haven't we seen this guy before?

I was in a state of shock as the unthinkable was becoming the
unfathomable.

They split the entire TV screen into EIGHT DIFFERENT
IMAGES OF ME CLAPPING from eight different shows. All
frozen images. Freeze-frames. Beards, sunglasses, baseball caps.

Suddenly one of the images takes over the screen. Another
infomercial. *Mr. Kim's Pocket Book Recipe for Wealth* and the free
bonus Never Get Lost Again Informative Compass. Jay Leno
decides it's best I explain it from my appearance on that show. The
tape rolls.

"Yes, I was lost once, and thank God for the Never Get Lost
Again Informative Compass, which guided me straight back home
while giving me interesting facts about the town I was in." "Never
knew Westmoreland County was George Washington's birthplace!"

The show then decided to put two separate images of me
(LAUGHING and CLAPPING) side by side splitting the screen.
In one I had a mustache, the other none. Through the magic of tel-
evision, they proceeded to POP A MUSTACHE on the clean-
shaven one proving they were both me. The same person. A fraud.
An impostor. Place wailed with laughter. Real laughter.

As I mentioned previously, my job was all about staying
anonymous. The faceless face of crappy late night television. I was
now being singled out on the highest-rated talk show on TV as the
guy you hire for just that. I would never be allowed to work again.

While I stood there in a state of utter dismay Chris called from his apartment. He was watching it, too. He'll be right over.

Jay Leno then decided to wrap the entire segment up. "So if anyone out there should know the whereabouts of who we are officially naming . . . THE CLAPPER!"

An obviously well-rehearsed horror musical shrill accompanies the words: *THE CLAPPER* across my FACE. He continues that if anyone should spot or know the whereabouts of me to please call into the show.

I was officially a wanted man.

Hopefully this'll all just blow over or something.

Chris comes over and we go to Astro Burger. This is our place to go and talk troubles, which seldom include massive television bounties on our heads. My head.

It's late. I feel people are looking suspiciously at me. Did they see the show? Are they gonna try and bring me in? Chris reminds me that people in Astro Burger at two in the morning don't look suspiciously AT, just plain look suspicious. This is true. I'm a bit paranoid. Keep tellin' myself this'll all just blow over, soon as they're on to the next skit. Has to.

Next morning we head to the Gower studios for three consecutive clapping gigs. Fifty dollars a pop. A show. One hundred fifty dollars will make a nice dent in my bills and another chip towards mine and Judy's wine dinner.

An old man stares as I approach the studio. I'd almost put the nightmare from last night out of my head. Nightmare of the Jay Leno segment. Woke up thinking, *That couldn't of really happened could it?*

Old man keeps staring. "You . . . from that show?" I get that a lot. Usually people NEVER figure it out. If you think remembering a game show host quickly walking by can be difficult, try remembering the guy who asked the retired game show host on the infomercial if "that stuff really gets tires squeaky clean." Near impossible.

Still it seems those moments lodge somewhere in peoples' minds though. Get questionably noticed all the time. Wasted information. Bowels of the psyche. Brain clutter.

Old man keeps staring.

OLD MAN

Yeah, that Jay Leno guy. You're that funny guy from it.
The CLAPPER!

Two other people, also gawking, joyously agree. "We knew we recognized you!" I glance and see Louise the producer waiting at the studio's gate.

If she saw me on that Jay Leno segment last night I'll never work again. My career here will be over. Everything I've . . . clapped for. I've been outed.

Too nice a day to get fired, I asked Chris to see if he could find out. "Tell her I got sick or something." "That I'll definitely be in tomorrow."

I went to the gas station. Lost out on the $150.

Haseem Karesh also works at the gas station.

It's too early for Judy to be at the station but I go anyway. I don't know. Wishful thinking.

Haseem Karesh is there. Works the day shift. He's the worst. Complete nightmare to deal with.

Chris says he speaks fluent "incorrectlish."

Have nothing against people who don't speak English but . . . well that must mean I do. I hope not but this guy drives me nuts.

I went to Mexico once. Tijuana. I know a little Spanish. *Pocito* ya know? Couldn't even imagine walking right up and speaking to someone. Too self-conscious. If I did, loud and assertively most certainly would not be the style. Always in fear of asking something in the world of, **"hello dog wall carpet?"**

Haseem's and my concerns certainly are different. Loud and assertive he certainly knows. Money he knows. Actually money's the only English he does know. A wordsman of sorts in the linguistics of currency.

It's like the guy went to "English payment methods speaking class only." Ask him anything and you'll get some form of payment response.

Knowing it's a waste I walk up and ask for Judy anyway. His reply, "American Express Visa pay now!"

I only know Haseem's name because he wears a patch on his shirt right beside a HUGE smiley face that reads "It's such a pleasure to serve you." Funny. Not just **"A"** pleasure. **"SUCH"** a pleasure. Always think of that old play on words from that *Twilight Zone* episode whenever I see it. Episode where these martians come down and leave a handbook behind that reads *To Serve Man*. A cookbook.

While standing there contemplating asking Haseem once again about Judy, a Chinese man beeps and yells more broken English from a car behind me at the station. His T-shirt reads "I LIKE TO SHIT!"

Looks about 45. Nice car. Probably a family man. NO way this guy knows what his shirt says. Might as well be walking around in one that reads "I Have No Idea *What* My Shirt Says!"

For this and a few other good reasons I don't speak or wear shirts in foreign languages. Too easy to make fool of "Round Eyes" with those pretty letters. Characters.

After a few more peeks around the station I couldn't resist. Had to ask Haseem again.

Seems American Express, Visa, and Mastercard are all still acceptable forms of payments there.

I head over to Astro Burger for a soda.

Dreams, inventions, hot phrases. A betamax store.

I'm full of good ideas. Well, ideas. You'd be surprised at the amount of intense think-tanking that goes on in places like Astro Burger. Middays, while the rest of the world is hard at work you'd swear cancer was being cured if you closed your eyes and listened to the madness being talked about in these booths.

Overheard a guy one night talking about this invention he was working on. Car that could actually fix its own blown tires while still driving. Elaborate. Meticulously calling out even the most minute details of it. "Dual layers" of some sort of foam rubber, an "inner airstream," sounded foolproof. When he mentioned the possibility of it being "three-dimensional" I turned and realized he was talking to his **FOOD.** Interesting idea nonetheless.

Doing crappy jobs alongside friends with long stretches of nothing can breed this sort of thinking as well. Great thing about being broke and on the verge of mental collapse is your mind goes straight to rocket ships and time travel. No one invents paper clips while piecing together change for a quesadilla.

Me and Chris have solved just about every world problem between tapings of *Judge Abrahms*, possible links between evolution and vegetables on a long day Clapping for the "Juice Man," and an obvious yet overlooked end to the oil crisis during set changes of various Leshko infomercials.

As for inventions . . . all it takes is one. Make a million dollars on it. One simple idea and you're set. One good one. No more working forever.

Chris had the idea of a shoe that actually GREW along with you. You could buy it for a kid and they could die of old age IN it. Unfortunately he came up with absolutely NO idea on HOW to make this shoe. Never mind the fact that people's taste probably changes between the ages of oh . . . one and ninety.

We did a show once on how to patent your ideas. "For ONLY $10,000 you, too, can patent ANYTHING!" My question (I got an extra $50 bucks for) was "I have a great idea for the pencil industry now that computers seem to be all the rage." "How can I go about getting a patent on this?" Always loved when the writers of these things tried to give it that extra touch of hip or something with lines like, "all the rage."

These infomercials can really screw your head up though. Watch them for their entire half hour (sometimes full hour) and you'll start to believe. They lull you in. You saw that movie *The Ring* right?

Just sit there staring. Thinking you're not taking it in. Next thing you know you got yourself a Veggie Slicer in four easy payments. Makes great-looking . . . radishes.

On the patent infomercial they went on to explain that every time you hear the "Happy Birthday" song someone's getting paid. Seems some shrewd business mind bought the copyright to it way back and's been laughing all the way to the bank ever since.

People copyright all sorts of things. Slogans like "Y2K," "Let's get ready to rumble!" Problem is, if you watch these shows long enough and have access to extra cash (luckily these two don't often go together) you just may find yourself dropping that mere $10,000 on a patent for such unforgettable catchphrases as "One Two Three . . . **FOUR!**" as opposed to "One Two Three!" "Isn't that a great idea?" No. It isn't.

Chris and Geronimo were on a roll after sitting through that infomercial. Good two weeks before you could even have a moment of peace around them. Slogan after slogan that made little, no, or non-sense. Geronimo's "Have Car Will Travel" seemed the most feasible to drop our $10,000 (that we didn't have) on, while "Soap of the Future" was Chris's. Remember, he didn't INVENT this soap of the future or ANY soap at all. Just the slogan "Soap of the Future."

I laugh but my ideas probably seemed as ridiculous to everyone as well. Luckily mine didn't need a patent.

Each paycheck I'd pay my bills and put a little aside for my wine dinner with Judy. With all my extra cash (yeah, ALL of it) I opened an account towards my own personal dream. A betamax-only video store. If there were any chance for me to have a future with Judy, I felt owning a store was a start.

I understand that probably sounds ridiculous. But I'd done my research on public library computers amongst all the other people you may have seen talking to themselves there.

Seems if you type "betamax" into the computer you get somewhere in the world of 582,000 sites. Millions of them were sold at one time. Where did they all go? Either way a million must still exist.

These people have had no way of renting movies for close to twenty years. A distributor (Mr. Assarat) in Cambodia still makes them with all the new titles. Actually had titles that weren't even released yet. A bit shady but well, he did call me back.

I found him on the Internet. Once a month I get a phone card to keep in contact with Mr. Assarat who's quite excited about branching out to America.

Found the perfect storefront on Ventura Blvd. It was previously a video store but Blockbuster opened across from it and it went under. Blockbuster doesn't sell betamax though. Doesn't rent them, either. No one does. You'd own the entire market. Me, Judy, and Chris. Anyone anywhere in America would be coming to you. Us. We'd have mail-ins, everything. There's this perfect area for a concession stand there as well. Fountain sodas. Popcorn with real butter ya know? Maybe get some fold-up chairs, show movies once a month or something. Make it a big night out at the betamax store.

Sometimes I get real worked up about it. Start thinking maybe I'm out of my mind, but something tells me this could be that ace in the hole, the big cash-in. Either way it's a dream. My dream. Everyone needs one. Envisioned even the way the letters should look on the awning. Me, Chris, and Judy all under the same roof.

I'm off drifting again. Sound of someone arguing about the Tuesday taco deal not being available today (it's Monday) brings me right back to reality. Astro Burger. 4 pm. Chris is done with his fries. A few still linger. "You done with those?" Take another sip of soda and ponder between two different styles of letters I'd been trying to decide on for that awning. Once, of course, this store opens. And we get one.

three dollars.

I love my job but sometimes it can get you down. When you actually think about it, you basically do nothing. I mean, yeah we clap and laugh I guess but well, Mondays can sometimes be a real drag. Work's been a bit slow the past week but we hear there's a whole bunch of unwatchable stuff coming in for us to sit and clap through next week. Nonetheless it can get you down.

I get home exhausted from these days of nothing. Nothing's like having three dollars in your pocket. Fifty or a hundred comes and goes like water. Three just sits around brewing and brewing. Nowhere to go. Don't wanna spend it. Not my last three. My days without work are three-dollar days. Long, monotonous, bland, unnerving. Time to go to the gas station and spend them.

Merry Christmas.

When I pull in, Judy's pulling an apron over her three-button shirt. I hop out of the car and run over. On line right in front of me is Mrs. Roper. Judy gets so excited she nearly drops Mrs. Roper's half gallon of milk. Who buys milk from gas stations?

We both laugh. As Mrs. Roper walks away, through the glass I ask for a carton of eggs and some chicken cutlets. She laughs and shushes me. Streets seem so empty. Judy reminds me it's the week of Christmas. "Oh yeah." Funny. Los Angeles and Christmas are a strange mix.

Well, that explains the slow work. I go to my hatchback, pull out my foldable beach chair.

Take a seat in the warm, not-so-lonely-anymore California Christmas weeknight. Pop a straw in my quart of Tropicana while Christmas music plays through static-ridden speakers over a mustardish moon . . . and away we go.

Eddie?

"Eddie?" I wake up in my chair. "Eddie?" For a minute I'm lost. Looks like the moon is talking to me. It's coming from the speaker system. Oh, the gas station. Look at my watch. 11:15 pm. Been sleeping out here for over an hour. Yes, Judy. "Oh, just checking if you were there." I'm here Judy, as I peek over at the box to let her know for sure. She smiles as I sit back down.

"Eddie, when you were a kid did you do that to your mother?" What? "Oh, just call her name in the night with no question hoping she'd peek in on you?" Yeah. Yes I did.

The unveiling.

I walk in to the television on. 11:45 PM.

JAY LENO
So our question of the day comes from . . . can we have
a drum roll please.

Across the entire screen **THE CLAPPER** appears in that
horrible green font again. Accompanying them are eight
separate images of ME in embarrassing-looking situations.
Some I'm frozen pointing, laughing. One I'm actually in midair
(a freeze-frame) jumping up and down on a "trampoline for
adults."

JAY LENO

Yes "The Clapper!" We dug into our vault again and came
up with yet another Clapper appearance. (Laughs) I mean
this guy . . . this guy's just great. You gotta watch this.

They cut to me on some infomercial asking a question about
keeping meat frozen. Some sort of "everlasting" ceramic wrap
that well, keeps meat frozen FOREVER. Horrible.

Jay Leno pointing me out on national television once again
basically is the death of my career. I'll never work again.
Maryanne or Louise see this and it's really over. Saving up for my
wine dinner with Judy now seems unattainable.

It seems these people have dug up endless video of ME from
all the infomercials and bad TV shows I've done. Nightmare. One
after another they're running footage. An ongoing punch line.

"You mean to say there are homes all over the world going
into foreclosure that I can buy for practically pennies?" Jay even
answers a few of my infomercial questions as part of his skit.

JAY LENO

Yes there Mr. Clapper. We have some huts in Somalia
you may be interested in.

The audience is eating it up.

In some I have fake beards, mustaches, sunglasses, my L.A.
Dodgers hat.

Not only is Jay pointing this out but EXPLAINING to the
audience (of millions) that "he's probably wearing these disguises to hide the fact that he's on every single one of these

shows!" My GOD! He's hit the nail on the head that incidentally just closed my coffin!

I imagine it doesn't get worse until he decides to cut to one of his infamous "Jaywalking" skits. These are the ones where Jay Leno "takes it to the streets." Speaks to the common man. This segment dedicated to, well, let's just say Jay's wearing a giant SANDWICH board that reads "Do You Know The Clapper?"

Seems he's figured out that Gower Studios is where the shows I clap for are filmed. He's standing right by a line of people waiting to see another late-night show. He's about 500 feet off. I know exactly where he is. The dogs are closing in. Surrounded by tourists who love the camera. "Clappers Gone Wild" remember?

He asks a few college kids who "don't know The Clapper but would love to meet him!" Flattering?

An old man walks by:

BOTHERED ELDERLY WHITE MAN
Don't know him. Don't care to. Just another silly plot
for some do-nothing to get his picture in the papers.

So it seems college students like me (think of trends such as Vietnamese potbellied pigs) while older people find me repulsive. All fine except for the fact none of them should know I exist. I watch Jay's crew slowly begin to move. Closing in. Things have gone from bad to awful, from unbelievable to unfathomable to . . .

JAY LENO
So you actually know The Clapper?

CHRIS

Well . . . yes but I don't think he's too happy about this.

Yes. Chris Plork. My lifelong friend turned informant. Seems Chris went to work today and was lured to the spotlight.

JAY LENO

Wait a minute. You actually know The Clapper and you're saying he has a *message* for us?

CHRIS

No, I mean.

JAY LENO

So please give us this message from The Clapper.

CHRIS

Well, the uh . . . Clapper . . . Eddie . . . is he doesn't . . . or the message. He wants to be OK to keep working on television shows.

It seems Jay and his crew eventually did move that extra five hundred feet over. Zeroed in, locked and secured the location. As luck (bad in this case) would have it, Chris ended up on camera as someone who actually knows this CLAPPER. Me.

JAY LENO

You mean to say The Clapper's, Eddie . . . is that his name? His message to "*the people*" is that he wants to continue working on television shows?

CHRIS

Message?

JAY LENO (on television)

Well you please tell The Clapper we'd love him to keep working on television shows. Now, can you lead us to him or is he in some . . . secret undisclosed location?

Audience is hysterical. Behind Chris I spot Geronimo just glowing with anticipation. Basking in the sun. Licking his chops at the opportunity to give me up for a mere twenty seconds of air time. Another page to his résumé.

I could almost feel the hesitation in my telephone's ring. Chris probably dialed a good six times before getting up the guts to ring it through.

Walk over to answer, as the recorded skit on my TV continues.

CHRIS (on television)

And he doesn't always have a mustache or beard. . . . Wow, he's not gonna be too happy about this.

Audience LAUGHTER.

Judas.

We met at Astro Burger.

How could he do this? Didn't he understand this would be the end of me? I had it all. Well . . . things were good. Saving up to take Judy out. Some on the side towards the dream. A job nobody bothered me at. An apartment with a TV, full refrigerator, and now this.

My oldest and closest friend had become my Judas. Promised to not go on again but the damage was done. I know Chris better than to think he did any of this consciously. He wouldn't and actually doesn't do much consciously. Regardless, THE CLAPPER is now a living breathing human being and Jay Leno has a direct link to him. My friend Chris Plork!

A producer from the show gave him a number. Said to call once he spoke to me. They'd love if I'd come on. Come on and do what? Clap?

In the background I spot some men on a scaffold posting a billboard. Maybe I could get a job doing that. Afraid of heights but I could probably deal.

All kinds of thoughts roll around my head as this billboard slowly begins unveiling itself. Moldy green in color. Ad for a horror movie? Starting to look familiar? How about this:

DO YOU KNOW THE CLAPPER?

Twenty-foot advertisement for the Jay Leno show going up on Santa Monica Blvd. So completely surreal I almost smiled. Said "almost" because I certainly did not.

Things were getting out of hand.

Santa Monica Blvd. at night.

I pull back in to Judy's gas station around 2 AM. She smiles. Surprised I'm back. Flicks on these funny Christmas lights she just installed on the roof. On and off. Head bobbing as if attached to her arm pulling a lever for them. Her laugh makes me smile. Makes me forget. Not just the madness with Jay Leno. All the bad stuff.

Judy's the girl you wait all your life for. Don't feel like you have to be anything but yourself around. Things at least for me get quiet when I'm around her. Peaceful. I like how that quiet feels.

Pull the beach chair back out from my trunk. Sit down. Hi Judy. "You're back!" Couldn't sleep.

I wanna tell her things. Things that shouldn't be said through an intercom but that's how we talk.

Look at that moon, huh?

She works nights. Never watches TV. No idea what's been going on. Fine with me. I could sit here for all eternity just talking back and forth. Funny how that goes.

Warm night. World just goes away here. Wouldn't stay away.

Confrontations with Emaciated Superheroes

Next day I'm walking with Chris down Hollywood Blvd.

Days of Bob Hope and Lucille Ball in this place are over. Seems the Walk of Fame got traded in long ago for runaways, dianetics, and misled tourists who'd like their money back.

We're headed to a marketing research gig. Never wanted to come back to these. Not because I didn't like them. Just really enjoyed Clapping.

Chris is a good friend. Calls in about these and comes along. Guess he enjoys being with me as much as I do him. Attached at the . . . somewhere I guess after all these years. If we were any more successful or better looking people'd swear we were gay.

Presently we're going to this one for a survey on BMW SUVs. Designed to help the manufacturers figure a way to target their consumers. BMW is certainly barking up the wrong tree. Seems not many people who can afford them these days are interested in spending the afternoon answering questions for $45. That's where we come in.

I've got on a fake beard and sunglasses due to the fact that at the present time I'm kind of famous. Not in any cool or even slightly redeemable way. I'm famous for being THAT GUY that laughs and claps at the garbage on your TV for cash.

Well, as I mentioned, Hollywood Blvd. is going (as my father would say) "down the drain." Sure sign of it is the cast of workers in front of the famed Mann's Chinese Theatre.

All sorts of almost recognizable comic book and Disney characters handing out flyers, charging $5 for a Polaroid with them.

I say "almost recognizable" because something's always slightly off. Whole area reeks of cease & desist orders.

Stick around long enough and you'll actually see lawyers "serving" people in crappy getups to STOP using characters' likenesses.

Saw a drunk Popeye once throw a DRACULA cape on his back in order to NOT be infringing on the Popeye estate's copyright. Loopholes in everything. Popeyeula I guess. Count Popeye. Horrible.

Pill-popping Marilyn *"Marlows"* posing with disappointed tourists right beside unkempt Charlie *"Chaplingtons"* nodding out in front of static-ridden microphones, holding flyers to various $1.99 Chinese food shops. Yeah, the place is nuts. Simply change a letter or part of a name and there you go. Legal. Law-abiding superhero . . . ish. Plagiarist-free.

It seems Marvel comics finally caught up with the EMACI-ATED looking Spider Man that was determined to fight his case to the end. Presently and unhappily going by "Insect Guy." Actually quite hateful about it. "Think any tourists want a photo with fucking Insect Man?"

Insect Man hangs with the always irritated SUPER MAN-ly and WONDER-ful WOMAN (a straight-up MONSTER).

These people, in NO WAY, represent any superhero that could save ANY-THING under ANY circumstance. They can, tell you to "go fuck yourself" if you ask them for directions. They do smoke (openly) and are drunk (often).

They work for themselves. Buy cheap costumes at Save-On Pharmacy around Halloween, hang crappy cameras around their necks and slap tourist children with harsh doses of reality. "Yeah, Super Man-ly ain't doing so good kid. Tell Mommy that'll be five dollars."

As I'm walking with Chris we see this guy dressed as a sandwich. Bottom of the food chain. Ha! Poor guy can barely see through all that hanging green fabric (lettuce).

Through this hanging lettuce though I see a glimmer in his eye. That look of almost recognition. More clear than usual though. I turned away and there it was.

A huge new *CLAPPER* billboard up on the Boulevard. HUGE. Stare for a moment and realize I'm wearing the exact same outfit in it (fake beard and sunglasses). Look back at the sandwich who's laughing and calling his buddies (other food people) over. Thought to walk on but instead reminded him that he was a meat sandwich.

Sandwich tells me not to get all "wound up." He's accompanied by a Darth Vader guy who obviously has yet to be spotted by the Star Wars franchise, being he still calls himself that.

Funny (or not, actually) he doesn't need a voice box to emulate the famous Darth Vader one because well . . . he's had a TRACHEOTOMY! No joke! Man's turned talking through a hole in his neck into a career. Yes, the glass can always be half full.

TRACHEOTOMY DARTH VADER
We were just saying you were pretty funny on Leno last night.

I let him know I wasn't trying to be funny. Wasn't trying to be anything. Certainly not Jay Leno's court jester. The emaciated Spider . . . INSECT MAN sarcastically jumps in:

EMACIATED INSECT MAN
Don't I get like a reward or something for bringing you in?

Before I knew it a crowd was gathering. Directly below a giant billboard of myself I stood there arguing with a cast of grown men in costumes, slowly being surrounded by tourists pointing fingers and whispering. One little boy informs his mother, "No that's the clap man mommy."

I rip off my beard and let the mother know her kid's right. I am the Clap Man. That's what I do. I Clap Clap Clap!

A HUGE crowd surrounds me. Trapped. I drop my beard as they grab for it like a pack of wolves. Fearing for my safety, my life, my . . . dignity's long gone. I ran.

Halfway down the block and out of breath I practically ran square into the Jay Leno "JAYWALKING" crew out filming another segment in search of Me.

I run down McAdden Lane into the nowhere again. Hopefully, nowhere still exists somewhere.

The television is once again on when I arrive home.

JAY LENO

Now you mean to say you just saw The Clapper and this is his beard?

FRANTIC WOMAN

Yes! He was just here. Yelling and dancing and . . . and CLAPPING.

TRACHEOTOMY DARTH VADAR

He was acting irrational.

AUDIENCE LAUGHTER

JAY LENO

Clapping? This guy doesn't seem to get enough. Can you tell me where he's gone or . . . ?

FRANTIC WOMAN

He just ran and . . . he dropped his beard here look!

JAY LENO

Yes I see. We seem to be closing in on him. (Looks into

camera) And just so you know . . . you can run, Clapper
. . . but you can't hide.

Man in crowd yells.

MAN IN CROWD

Put a bounty on him Jay!

ANOTHER MAN IN CROWD

Dead or alive!

Chris comes up with a plan.

At night my dreams (nightmares) are filled with HOR-
RIBLE visions of Judy partaking in various orgy-fests with well-
equipped versions of the EMACIATED INSECT GUY. Betamax
stores opening by the dozens selling CLAPPER merchandise.
Slow-motion chase scenes with the Sandwich Man. Awful.

Phone rings. Whew, glad someone woke me outta that. But
then again . . . now I'm IN THIS (reality).

Chris, on the other end, asks what's wrong. Never asks things
like that. I must sound terrible. Explain my nightmare. How everyone
in it was making out like bandits. How I was getting nothing.

Chris offhandedly brings up the idea of asking the show for
money. Turning myself in for some sort of reward. A sort of

bounty on myself. Did Chris actually just come up with the greatest idea of our lives? I look to him with astonishment. He's fallen asleep on the other end. I think.

A million dollars.

I yell for about ten minutes into my receiver as Chris snores
on the other end. He wakes and asks why I called. Sure.

I ask him for that producer guy's number again. Better yet I'm
gonna write a note. Chris will deliver it directly to the studio.

Tell the show I'll agree to come on as a guest if they pay me.
Chris says that's a great idea.

We go back and forth with a fair price. Chris starts with $50.
I start with a million.

If they go for this we're set. A million dollars is . . . A MIL-
LION DOLLARS! Along with daydreaming of inventions and
solving world problems on coffee breaks, the term "million dollars" is synonymous with horrible crappy jobs.

Nowhere else on earth will you hear it used as much as between workers in low-paying awful jobs on downtime. It's the magic number. Means not only will you NEVER have to work again but you're legitimately rich. A Millionaire. Rich people think more specifically. Tax free? Increments?

Knowing it's just a pipe dream we'd keep it simple. One million dollars.

And here I am with the possibility of grabbing that pipe dream.

I grab a pen and begin my note.

Dear Jay Leno . . .

The zeros get confusing so I cross them out and write the words. Chris will personally deliver this to him tomorrow.

The delivery.

Next morning Chris walks through the NBC lobby where he's confronted by Ralph Ranter. Ranter's the producer Chris met out on the street. Tells him he has a note for Jay. Ralph immediately opens it. Practically salivating he asks Chris to follow him to the green room (where important guests of the *Tonight Show* wait). His eyes are electric. Sees something in the note. A deal? If I'da been there I'd of sworn this was a good sign. It wasn't.

Ralph Ranter (nice ring to it huh?) sits Chris alongside a juggler and Simon Cowell from *American Idol*. Asks him to wait a minute and rushes out.

A giant tray of sushi separates Chris from Simon Cowell.

Directly down the hall an entirely different situation was at hand.

Ralph Ranter had called an emergency meeting with some fellow producers, the show's lawyer (Horatio), and Jay Leno himself. Was this to discuss the million dollars? The end of bad jobs? A life without worry?

LAWYER HORATIO

Either way the legalities . . . We can't be just giving away money blatantly over the air for people to basically turn themselves in to us.

RALPH RANTER

Why not?

LAWYER HORATIO

Because that's immoral and . . . I mean, can't we give him a stove or something?

During sick-from-school afternoons with my mother as a kid I remember watching shows like *Let's Make a Deal* and *The $10,000 Pyramid.* Got all excited about a couple winning a washer and dryer once. My mother felt the need to explain. (Squash the Easter Bunny, kill Bigfoot.) "When these pedestrians" (she ALWAYS harshly called ANY contestant on a game show a pedestrian) "win things like this, they get hit with harsh taxes backstage and (laugh) wait til they see their next electric bill!" "Be wishing they never met that goddamned Bob Barker!"

Yeah, she wasn't too big a fan of the radical front five rows of costume wearers on *Let's Make a Deal*, either. "A grown man dressing as a tin can is an abomination!"

Well, I certainly didn't want any prizes from the Jay Leno show. This "pedestrian" wanted his million dollars.

I waited for Chris to come back from NBC with the good news. Had it all worked out? Like the office-maintenance guy in the Lotto pool I'd already gone and spent the whole million in my head.

Chris left at noon. No word yet. Two becomes three becomes five became eight pm. Still no word. Don't dare leave the house in case he calls. No other way to make contact.

9 pm

They wouldn't have killed him right? Of course not. Ridiculous. He wouldn't have taken the cash and run off, either. Puerto Rico?

10 pm

Mind is racing. Visions of those old subway Bacardi ads are everywhere. Chris, beachfront in Puerto Rico. Breaded-and-fried everything. A million in cash all stacked beside him.

11:30 pm

11:35. Still no Chris. Something's terribly wrong. Must had called his answering machine fifty times. It's full of questions from me. Put on the Jay Leno show because, well, that seems to be where I get all my information these days.

JAY LENO
And here he is ladies and gentlemen. Our very own "Deep Throat," Chris Plork!

The audience applauds as Chris walks out like he's being led blindfolded. Completely discombobulated. Picture, Pin the Tail On the Donkey. WHAT THE HELL IS HE DOING ON TELEVISION?

Visions of Mr. Magoo riding his car up the roller coaster. "These hills are just ridiculous Cha-lee."

He's introduced as "the messenger of The Clapper's initial demands."

As the audience chuckles away, my suspicions are confirmed. Chris has no idea how or why he's out there. Just is. Jay asks he read my latest demand (the note) live on the show.

Plan was simple. Chris delivers my note to Jay Leno and leaves. Possibly with a check but most likely they'll think it over. Maybe negotiate us down a bit.

Him appearing ON the show was NOT part of ANY piece of this plan. Chris hesitantly obliges.

CHRIS (*reading*)

It also seems to me that you would like to meet in person on your show. I do not know what you normally pay your guests. I know some will not go on no matter how much you offer them. However, I am broke and would be very happy to appear on your show for ~~1,000,0000000~~ 1 million dollars.

While the audience is busy laughing, gasping, I'm appropriately looking for a hole near a rifle to stick and blow my head off at the same time.

I had enclosed one of my fake mustaches for proof so they

would know we were serious. Doesn't seem to exactly be translating "serious" as Jay dangles it to the howling laughter of a packed unpaid audience.

Plan seems to have gone by way of the toilet. Pronounced *terlitt* by my Brooklyn-born mother.

The Telephone Rings

Chris knows he screwed up. Knows he did big time. He's not retarded. Hate that word but you gotta admit this is some retarded shit. In all fairness I know that look he gets though (blindfolded-walk one). Seen him led out enough times on infomercials to recognize it. Unwilling trance or old-lady-hypnotized-on-the-*Ed Sullivan-Show* look. Very 1950s sci-fi.

I know it isn't his fault. Nonetheless we're screwed. Besides the million dollars lost we've probably broken some laws as well.

I was attempting to hold myself hostage and had the ransom note read over the airwaves. Something's gotta be illegal about that I imagine.

Ask me if I'm a fireman.

OK, are you a Fireman?

No.

I'm driving to see Judy at the gas station. It's late. Always late. 11 pm Santa Monica Boulevard.

AM radio has some guy talking about the power of suggestion. They mention me. Unbelievable. Debating how "my field" (I get $45 a show for being at the forefront of this field) is corrupting and misleading the general population. Man hosting this debate has a VERY low and slow radio tone to him.

AM RADIO TALK SHOW HOST

And what this brings to light is the manipulative power
of suggestion. For example let's try a joke. Ask me if
I'm a fireman, Hilda. Yes, a fireman. Ask me if I'm one.

RADIO GUEST HILDA

Are you a fireman?

AM RADIO TALK SHOW HOST

No.

Host then blasts a loud laugh track. Infectious. Can't help but
crack a smile from my car. Suddenly he shuts it off. Silence.

AM RADIO TALK SHOW HOST

Well, sorry to break this to you Hilda but there isn't a
single thing funny about that joke. I was simply stating the
obvious. No, I am not a fireman. I work at a radio station.
Host of this very show you're on right now. Not one iota
of humor in there. Yet accompanied by a laugh track . . .

The world has gone insane. Can't put on the television, radio
. . . I'm getting noticed in the supermarket. Can't work. Seems
while everyone is debating my influence on society I can't pay my
phone bill.

It's an awful feeling I have today.

My refuge, as it's always been, is Judy.

I run out of gas just as I pull up to her station. Cruise on
empty to a slow halt five feet from a pump. Get out to push as it
starts raining. Appropriately. The sky is falling.

Judy Has Legs

When you run into a teacher or someone you work with out of their element it can be really weird. Like, wow, you exist. Sometimes it can actually be kind of embarrassing.

Ran into my dentist once at a club, drunk. Felt like I walked in on him showering naked or something. Uncomfortable. Like, aren't you always looking at teeth?

I'd never seen Judy outside of that box. Never even occurred to me she didn't sit in that chair behind that glass and talk through a speaker all the time.

As I pushed my car, there she was. Waiting for a light to turn green in the rain. Patiently pressing the "cross" button.

Almost turned away as if I was breaking some sort of rule. Awkward. Kind of exciting as well. I mean, I'd only seen half of her before. Waist up. Through a glass.

Oblivious to the rain all I could think was that I'd never seen her legs before. Knew she had them (legs), I guess. Just never thought of it.

Ran over accidentally startling her. She dropped her *Catcher in the Rye* book in a puddle. I felt awful. Apologized til I realized she was soaking wet. We were soaking wet. Oh yeah, it's pouring.

Said she got a late-night lunch break now and was headed across to Astro Burger. Was taken back for a moment hearing her voice not coming through a speaker. Got a little more drenched trying to find the words to ask if I could join her til she invited me along.

She's nervous like I am. The good kind. It was as if we'd both just met again.

Got on a long line of late-night Astro Burger customers. Probably apologized about that book twenty times. Tells me she's read it a hundred times. Dropped it in two hundred puddles. I agree it's a great book even though I hadn't read it. Felt I probably should have. Know bits and pieces from Chris. He loves it as well. Calls it the anti-bully book. Must be powerful, as it seems to bring people's personalities to the forefront whenever on display.

Remember Chris leaving it on one of the marketing job's sign-in tables once. Strange watching the strong and telling reactions it provoked. Ernie, a fellow marketeer, volunteered that it didn't make a bit of sense to him. Nothing made sense to Ernie. Louise the producer called it a bunch of "horseshit."

Judy says it's a beautiful book that makes her cry. "Holden (the main character) is so sad and no one knows it."

The world really went away with Judy. Just thinking, writing about her I have to say her name. Judy. My heart belongs to her and she has no idea.

Heart's got your sleeve.

I'm gun-shy with emotions. There's this Jack Nicholson movie I recently saw where he's always writing e-mails to, I think, Diane Keaton. Afraid to let her know his real feelings, he constantly erases and replaces them with more formal messages. Made me think of Judy. Actually made me think of my mother.

Years ago I saw another movie where the message was something about making sure you let your parents know you love them before it was late.

Took the cue and sent my mother a letter. Nothing too dramatic. Simply, Ma I love you. Always wanted you to know that.

Three days later, upon receiving this letter she called to ask if I was suicidal.

Explained to her that just because a son tells his mother he loves her doesn't mean he's thinking of killing myself.

She agreed and asked if I was taking drugs.

The date.

So many words and feelings sit on the tip of my tongue as I watch Judy shyly wipe the rain off her hat on the Astro Burger line. Occasionally she'll look up with a smile as she does it. Almost apologetically. Points to it and reminds me it's rain.

Fish in my pockets praying for a twenty. Ten would cut it but a twenty would mean we could have anything and as much of it as we wanted.

A twenty! Anything Judy wants. She offers to pay. You kidding? I've been thinking about this since the minute I met her. She was wearing one of those nice shirts with a crocodile on it. Complimented her and some schmuck correctly pointed out that it was an alligator. Fine with me. I got the date at Astro Burger.

Judy says she'd like an orange soda. Along with people named Mabel and Lester, coconut custard pie, eight-track tapes, and betamax machines, orange and grape soda just sorta disappeared one day.

We decide to sit outside in the rain. Under the big white umbrellas shielding the tables and now us. Hot winds are blowing. Santa Anas. Sounds romantic. Even better, sounds fun.

She gets a table while I order that new Double Cheese Pleaser for 2. But for one ya know? And then two of them. So like four.

Throw in an orange soda for her and a grape for me. I imagine the guy preparing the orders in the back would be like "orange and grape?" Maybe even get a laugh out of it. Then I look at that guy in the back who didn't have much of an expression at all. Unfazed. Yeah well, frying french fries all day can probably do that to ya.

I head back to Judy.

Her eyes sparkle when she sees all the food. Made me smile. Everyone loves a full tray of food.

An orange for you and a grape for me. Welch's grape. Man, that's good stuff. Very Mayberry-ish. Opie-esque.

We decide that every Tuesday we're gonna do this on her new lunch break. 11 pm. Maybe even go somewhere else. Switch it up.

Tells me she's worried they might be cutting back at the station. Laying people off. I remind her that getting gas is usually just getting gas. Without her who would come?

Out of the blue (actually black night) a man darts by naked. Completely. Not a stitch of clothing. He's yelling but doesn't seem to be in any kind of real danger or distress. Well, for a man running naked in the rain that is.

Judy's got a hamburger bite halfway in her mouth as she looks over wide-eyed, smiling and mumbles out that she knows him. "That's Naked Larry." Gets the bite down, clears her throat and tells me she sees him all the time. His wife left him six months ago and this makes him feel better. "Asks for water every once in a while." Takes another bite and clears her throat again. Wants to tell me something.

JUDY

Sometimes it's kind of embarrassing working there at the gas station ya know?

Never even occurred to me she could feel that way. I mean, I could understand. Not that there's anything wrong with it. I'da fell for her on an unemployment line. I just understand. All my life I'd walked that thin line between trying to maintain and complete humiliation. Humbling to say the least. Probably why most people get so bitter. If not bitter you could spend your whole life sad. A sad sack.

As I go on attempting to fill every bit of uncomfortable air attempting to explain the depth of my understanding she jumps in.

JUDY

You know why I do? Why I work there? I don't know, it's like no one can find me. I mean, not like I'm hiding. More of well, at night no one's around, and especially on a night like tonight when it's raining. It's like I'm nowhere. But everyone's nowhere on a night like tonight right? You understand don't you?

I only nodded. Squeezed out a yeah. Of course I understood. Almost on cue "It Never Rains in Southern California" came on over the loudspeaker. What a funny song to come on when it's raining here.

The Nicest Thing Anyone's Ever Said to Anyone.

Before I could get too analytical or melancholy about what Judy had said she jumped up with an enthusiasm I'd never seen in her. It was contagious.

"I . . . I got a coupon last week for a free Thai massage for two on Sunset Blvd., wanna go?"

I thought to tell her it was probably like a hooker place or something when she caught my vibe. "Nah, not that kind!" Said she talks with one of the people who works there. An old guy from Thailand who says he walks on stilts on people's backs. "Real nice guy. Always leaves candy for tips when he gets gas."

Off of Sunset Blvd. around Western there's a small Thai community. I know how played out any sort of Elvis joke may be at this point but we peek into a place with a Thai Elvis that certainly was pretty good. Together we laughed and walked into a small mysterious mini-mall. All sortsa unwanted junk in it starting with a 97 cent store. I guess having one up on the 98 one across the street and two on the 99 off Van Ness Blvd.

Upon first walking in you're greeted by a very nice older lady selling soaps and all kinds of strange incense. We present the coupon. She smiles and calls, "Sam."

We're led into a back room filled with strangely placed Thai music. We're laid alongside each other separated by big white harem tents (curtains). Sam comes in with me, as Janice (yes, strange name for a Thai lady I know) goes in with Judy. Through the tents, Judy unexpectedly takes my hand. Holds it. When Janice and Sam step out to get us free tea, Judy lifts the curtain, peeking and smiling to say a simple "Hi."

Quickly closing the tents like two teenagers flirting behind their parents' backs I hear a giggle from her as a hundred-year-old NAKED Thai man runs by yelling.

Sam tells me the old man is "crazy," as he mistakenly swirls the finger gesture for crazy around his face instead of head. "Run back and forth, back and forth from hot water to cold, back and forth." Seems he really is a HUNDRED (turned it two weeks ago according to Sam)! "Say it makes long life." Seems to be working. The massage begins as Sam gets on stilts and walks on my back. It doesn't hurt, exactly. Well, a little.

When it's over they bring us tea and oranges. Judy looks

under the curtain. Reminds her and me both of the Leonard Cohen song. I sit for a minute, content. Happy. It's very nice. I don't feel like this often.

Sam says he's gonna put something special on for us. Over the speakers he replaces the soothing Thai music with Leonard Cohen's "Suzanne." How very strange and beautiful.

With all the mysticism of this special moment Judy peeks under the curtains again. Holding them with two hands like a habit over her head.

JUDY

I'm gonna tell you something OK? About two weeks ago some guy came by at around two in the morning wearing a TV on his head. It actually worked!

I asked, How? Was it battery operated? That's hysterical.

JUDY

All I could think of was how I wished you were there to see it with me. That's when I knew.

For the first time in my life I wasn't scrambling to fill a conversation. Not trying to avoid hearing the next part of someone's sentence. The part I knew would let me down.

JUDY

My mother used to . . . well she used to believe in UFOs right? When she'd put me to sleep at night, when I was little, she'd say, "I hope I never see a spaceship without you Judy." I thought that was the nicest thing anyone could ever say to someone.

She just looked at me after she said that. Nothing else. Told her that was a beautiful thing to say to someone. She kept looking. No words. Suddenly realized that is a beautiful thing to say to someone and it was being said to me. Leonard Cohen was repeating the line, "and you know that she's half crazy, but that's why you wanna be there."

We will meet each week at this time for a special date just like this one until we decide to meet more often.

Cindy Crawford

I'm not a very good joke teller and if I remember correctly, this isn't a very good joke.

I forget punch lines, important bits of information. Halfway through I'll be like . . ."oh did I mention the guy was blind?"

Well, there's this one about some guy on a desert island who gets one wish. He uses it for Cindy Crawford. Joke's obviously a bit dated as I'm sure there are more current supermodels to choose from. Anyway, after a year he gets another one and wishes for a guy. Any guy.

The Wishmaster, or whoever grants these things in jokes, wonders if he's turned gay. Grants him his wish.

First thing he says to the guy when he appears is "You'll never believe who I've been having sex with!"

Yeah, I don't get it entirely, either. Other than the fact that if you don't have someone to share things with it's just not as good.

I called Chris all night. Fell asleep and tried again. Went to his apartment around three the next afternoon and woke him up. Never understood people who could sleep that late.

Told him he'd never guess who I went on a date with until I realized he never would so I told him.

Noticed his answering machine blinking. Fifteen messages. "That Jay Leno producer guy's been calling all night." I ask if they agreed to pay us the money. "Didn't say anything about the money, except they aren't gonna press charges or anything for the ransom note."

Unbelievable. These guys make a laughingstock outta me, cost me my job, won't pay me, and now "*they*'re not gonna press charges on *me*!"

CHRIS

I think they want you to be a guest or . . . he said it would be good for . . . I don't know, something. It's on the messages.

The Voice Changing Machine.

Me and Chris have a whole assortment of strange things laying around our apartments. Go to a doctor or mechanic's place you'll probably find misplaced stethoscopes or tools. Being we're in the business of "being" ANYBODY, we have everything.

Accessories, disguises, IDs, all kinds of official-looking gear. FBI wandered into one of our places it'd make headlines.

As Clappers we have to blend in. As market research people we have to BE people. Sometimes important people. We do crazy stuff. Sometimes it's fun, sometimes we can't believe the predicaments we've gotten ourselves into.

On some of our Clapper gigs they'd ask us to be people as

well. Sometimes just interested audience members, sometimes participants, one time a mafia informant. It was on some terrible sort of Maury Povich ripoff show.

They chose Chris to sit behind a cloth barrier to disguise his face. Funny, being we do that anyway. I guess in a way they were disguising him the same way we do. Disguised from anyone who might realize he's NOT who they're saying he is.

They attached this voice changing machine to his shirt to supposedly "conceal" his identity. Said he was in the witness protection program.

Being Chris isn't exactly known for his enunciation, this basically made him completely unintelligible. They asked him scripted questions which he answered wrong being he couldn't read the paper they hung on the supposed cloth barrier.

When the show aired, being his answers were so completely inaudible, they typed out (in subtitle form) whatever they wanted them to be across the TV screen anyway.

When he got home that day the voice changing machine was still attached to his shirt. Forgot to take it off. From time to time he'll hook it up and call me. Chris can be quite a joker every year or so.

What to do with a voice changing machine.

Saw a cartoon once where they put one of those thought bubbles over a monkey. Milk carton + photo of banana = lightbulb flashing. Then, tree + photo of banana = lightbulb flashing. They went on and on pushing the point that ANYTHING + banana = lightbulb flashing for a monkey. Funny.

I like using monkey analogies. So as I sat in Chris's apartment thinking up equations that would = money (lightbulb flashing) I noticed that voice changing machine.

Wanted to call the producer of the Jay Leno show and get it straight. Were they gonna pay me or not. Just didn't want them to be able to record me or . . . I don't know, anything.

The machine would keep me anonymous. Sort of. I guess.

Getting Jay Leno or one of his producers on a call is something a lot of crazy people seem to want to do. Because of this they gave Chris a password for when he called that would put him directly on with Ralph Ranter (the producer).

Chris, of course, lost this password but recalled it to be something about a Musician calling a Clapper "or something."

I plugged in the voice machine, which after living in Chris's closet so long sounded more like a kid's broken walkie-talkie and called in.

Got hung up on three times by the receptionist who thought the machine was some kind of prank. I shut it off.

This is the Musician calling Mr. Ranter about the Clapper. She paused. "Can you repeat that?" "Are you sure you don't mean Magician?" Yeah, sure.

Next I know, I'm on with Ralph Ranter.

With the machine back on I tell him who I am. He's beside himself with excitement. Asks me to hold while he gets Jay Leno. Quickly adds that the sound of my voice is "a nice touch." "They'll love it."

That night on the Jay Leno show:

JAY LENO

Ladies and gentlemen this wasn't planned. But here, at
this very moment we have The Clapper on the line. I'm
gonna pick up here and . . .

Seems I called just as taping for the show began. Ralph made an executive decision to patch me through to Jay and his audience live on the air.

Being I had called them they could legally do this without asking my permission or even my knowledge of it taking place. I had no idea.

To explain what appeared (unbeknownst to me) on my television that night is complicated. I'd prefer to simply transcribe and let you figure it out.

Had to buy this transcription from the show for $10.

I'm "ME."

JAY LENO

Yes. Mr. Clapper . . . is it OK if I call you that?

ME (VOICE MACHINE)

Sure.

JAY LENO

So Mr. Clapper, that's some voice you have there. Very reminiscent of *Ransom* with Mel Gibson.

ME (VOICE MACHINE)

It's a voice changing machine.

JAY LENO

Well I'm relieved to hear that. So there's some kind of message or demand I'm told you wanted to make to me personally?

Mind you, the audience is laughing throughout this entire conversation.

Knew I heard something funny in the background when I called, just wasn't sure what it was. Actually thought it was this guy down the hall's dogs barking (they're always barking).

ME (VOICE MACHINE)

Well, sure . . . yeah. I mean, not really so much a demand. More of like, well, I was thinking, asking for a million dollars to come on your show might have been a bit much.

JAY LENO

You know, I imagine this has got to be the most polite conversation anyone's ever had with someone using a voice changing machine.

As the audience continued to laugh in the background (dogs continued to bark) I told him I'd cut my request significantly down to $100,000. At that point my machine cut off. Batteries ran out. Show was in an uproar as Jay made some sort of joke about Energizer or something.

That night I watched the show as it all unfolded. I was now not only a joke, but a willing participant in the bafoonerizing of myself.

The scent of the Clapper has been lifted.

Didn't seem to be much I could do about the situation so I went to sleep. Sort of.

One in the morning I get a call from Ralph Ranter. Opens with a laundry list of facts about me. Sounds like something out of a bad cop show. (EVERYTHING at this point is comparable to television.)

Got your number from your lifelong friend Chris Plork. Real name's Edward Krumble, born Queens, New York, moved here in '99. Worked under a fake social security number to avoid paying taxes on your Clapping gigs.

After assuring me he could care less what I do "legal or illegally"

he asks if I'd be willing to appear on the show. Tosses a complimentary comparison between my popularity and that of David
Letterman's Stupid Pet Tricks. If, of course, you would consider
this a compliment.

He instructs me, in full TV cop mode, to look out my window
at the Town Car they have waiting for me. I peer through the shade
as he tells me a room (all expenses paid) is waiting for me at the
Hilton in Burbank where they'd love me to spend the night and
prepare for an appearance on tomorrow's show.

I asked if that meant they'd agree to the $100,000. He reiter-
ated the show's policy that they could not and would not pay
guests to be on the air. The exposure though, he assured me could
lead to much greater things.

A BANG on the door nearly gives me a heart attack. I envi-
sion producers with stun guns and butterfly nets apprehending
me. Pinning a giant sign on me with an arrow

→ *this guy can't pay his bills!*

I quickly hang up the phone and see Chris through the peek
hole. It's 1:30 in the morning. Tells me Ralph Ranter called and
said to meet there. "Said they were bringing us to some all
expense place or something."

Yeah, "at my expense place."

I tell him they're attempting to kidnap and put us on display.
Break it down in Chris terms. "You saw *Planet of the Apes* right?"

I hop out the bathroom window and ask him to stay put. I'll
call once I get somewhere or, think of something or . . . ya know?

3 am at the Sunset Paradise Motel

Chris Rock said a joke once about what a nice thing our government did in honoring Martin Luther King by putting his name on the worst street corners of every major city in America.

Names can be deceiving.

When looking for a place to sleep, "Paradise" may sound good but it seldom means that. Trust me.

Surrounded usually by bail bondsman, pawn shops, liquor stores, and amputees.

Flashing neon lights declaring "Paradise" should be looked on as nothing short of a straight-up warning.

I call Chris who informs me he was nice enough to let a film crew into my apartment with their cameras. When I asked what they could have possibly said that would convince him that would be a good idea. He thought and replied . . . "well, they asked."

Ask and you shall receive from Chris. He's good like that.

4 am lecture on the power of the household appliance.

I pick Chris up and we head to the gas station. He tells me Ralph Ranter has now upped his offer from no money and public humiliation to household appliances and my ability to "plug" anything I wanted if I come on. Says they pay people by allowing them to promote things. If I were promoting being an idiot I'd of hit the jackpot.

These shows really are incredible. So cheap. Jim Carrey (the comedian) once reenacting how he believed awards shows were probably conceived. "Hey I have an idea, why don't we invite a bunch of famous people to be on our show and give them a piece of metal." "Long as we tell 'em it's a prize they'll do it for free."

I probably shouldn't use quotes but you get the idea. TV shows love paying you with appliances and gifts. They get it all free. Actually, at times they even get paid to pay you with this stuff. A real racket.

I'm on and on about this again with Chris. He barely listens. I'm exhausted. Judy'll understand.

4:15. Haseem's in the box.

We pull into the station. Haseem Karesh is in the booth. Payment methods guy, remember? I ask for Judy. He mutters an intelligible "gas credit card in machine or cash?"

What a shock huh? I tell him it's Judy's night. Why's he working the night shift? His response is something in the area of "Judy is for gas out pay."

Yeah. Guess you can call that progress. He did acknowledge her name before returning to his comfort zone in the English language. Doesn't help me any though.

Think to ask again. Judy's always here at this hour. Is she sick? Through the glass I see Haseem practically licking his chops. Like a dog sizing up a steak. Can't wait to drop another synonym for currency on me.

I almost want it. What's it gonna be? That all you got? How 'bout Diner's Club cards? You take them?

Instead I just leave. I'm a better man for it.

The manual Kool-Aid Polygraph tests.

Barely slept wondering why Judy wasn't at work. Long as I can remember she was always there. Never a sick day. Never even sick far as I knew.

I'm headed with Chris to a discreet and unmemorable area in the Valley. North Hollywood. Sounds nice. It's not.

Baron wasteland for aging almost-been actors stuck on what seems to be an extended pilot-season hiatus.

An indication of where we are could best be summed up by the marquee hanging on the theater across the street.

Every Thurs. thru Sunday in August Charles Nelson Reilly
in a lighthearted spin on *All That Jazz!*

We're headed for a marketing research job testing new and unproven polygraph machines. Actually, to have them tested on us.

I'm broke. Completely. Pays $45.

Place is depressing as hell.

Where there's usually a working coffee machine lies a broken coffee machine. Right beside it, a giant jug of warm Kool-Aid.

Poor Kool-Aid. Was a time it was the kids' choice. Remember "Hey Kool-Aid"?

Now it just conjures up negative . . . bad things all around. Mass suicides in Guyana, some book about mixing it with acid, and you just know it can't be good for you.

Along with Tang, Hi-C, and Hawaiian Punch there's just a big dark cloud over all of them now. Must be a '70s thing.

Something about that Kool-Aid jug though. Look at it. Just sitting there. Handle a bit broke. It's mere presence. Depressing the heck out of me.

A makeshift handwritten sign hangs on the door:

Polygrph Marketing Research through this door $45.

Yeah, I know Polygraph is spelled wrong. Bothered me, too. Something about that, the Kool-Aid jug, and $45 was just a real downer. Couldn't it have been $50? Even $40. A rounded-out number? An even one? Clean? The five really got to me. Somehow told me they had agreed on the lowest possible amount they could possibly get away with.

I needed cash though. Rent was coming, phone bills. Most importantly the wine date with Judy. Even the savings on the betamax dream had to be put on hold. Something I never wanted to do. Man needs a dream.

From what we've been told about this researching gig, they're going to strap us to these newly developed lie detectors to see how accurate they are. Fact that every single person . . . wait, let me look around . . . yup every single person here's a liar (recognize them all from when I was doing this circuit). I'll rephrase that. Being everyone here will be lying well, I imagine the results may vary. No one cares though. I miss my job and life as an audience member dreaming of owning a video store.

Half an hour later, forty-five dollars richer and eight hundred and . . . sixty-five dollars in debt I pull the car over with Chris. There's got to be some kind of way to at least be making our rents off this whole Jay Leno thing.

Chris hands me Ralph Ranter's number and a quarter. Hop out to a pay phone and tell the receptionist it's the magician and the Clapper whatever. She puts me through. Ranter picks up. Tell him I've had enough. No more jokes. I need cash. If they even want me to consider not straight-up disappearing they'll have to come up with some, any kind of way of paying me. I back down a bit as always. A sucker. Can't I drink a Coke or something on the show "won't that at least get me a hundred bucks?" Suddenly Jay Leno's on the line.

In the faint background I hear those dogs again. Ones that sound strangely like a laughing audience. They're broadcasting this! Quarter runs out and we're disconnected.

Get back in the car and look over at Chris. He's itching incessantly. Peels a patch off his chest. He's back to doing the guinea pig research. Twenty-five dollar cosmetic tester patches to see what makes grown men break out in hives.

No. Todays aren't supposed to be worse than yesterdays. Gotta go see why Judy was out last night.

The cordial attendant.

I hesitate, pause, check the street sign to be sure I'm at the right place. Judy's Island (the box she's usually in) is freshly painted. Blue and white. Sign's fixed. This all since yesterday.

A real college-y looking well-dressed guy sits upright. I ask real loudly when Judy will be in. Quite audibly and cordially he replies she's been let go.

Says he didn't know her but was told she'd been fired. Any further information would have to be obtained through the night manager Mr. Haseem Karesh. I tell him I already know how to use credit cards. He laughs (I guess he'd already picked that much up about the guy).

This is no laughing matter though. I want to know where Judy is.

Before I can continue my ranting an older guy on line recognizes me from the Jay Leno show. Cordial attendant's eyes light up, "I knew I knew you!"

Comes out to take a photo of me for his booth. I remind him he's in Judy's booth and storm off.

Something worth promoting.

Couldn't believe she'd been fired. Walked aimlessly around the station. The block. Astro Burger. How will I ever find her? No phone number, not even a last name. Know she lives somewhere in Sherman Oaks but that's a big place. I have no address. Always meant to ask for it but . . . she's always there.

Get home around 12:30 in the morning. Put the TV on and there it was.

JAY LENO (*on TV*)
Here he is everybody. Promoting the new single "Love and Mercy," off his first album in over ten years. Brian Wilson!

Something worth promoting.

BRIAN WILSON (*singing*)
I was sitting in a crumby movie with my hands on my
chin . . .

I envisioned somewhere in this big giant city Judy watching
as well. This was our song.

Next morning bright and early me and Chris are in the NBC
studios lobby. Ralph Ranter approaches like a kid in a candy store.

RALPH RANTER
Hello Chris. And you must be . . .

We're here to promote a search for Judy.

Yeah, that's me, Eddie. The Clapper I guess.

I'm fully incognito. Scarf, glasses, wig, beard. The whole
deal. I feel strangely important. Ranter introduces me to the
show's lawyer (Horatio) who quickly reminds me there will not
be any monetary payment for this. Before he can finish, Ranter
adds that of course there will be a goody bag (free soaps and
stuff), some giveaway prizes (tax-shelter microwaves or lug-
gage), and that yes, I certainly can promote that I would like this
mysterious . . . (looks at paper) "Judy girl to contact you through
our show as soon as possible." Knowing this is my only motiva-
tion for being here (and that it won't cost them a dime) he men-
tions it twice.

According to Ranter, Jay will sit with me for a minute or two in what Chris calls the free sushi room (green room), discuss a few things and we'll be off and running. The off and running part makes me a bit nervous.

JAY LENO

And now, ladies and gentlemen without further ado may I please introduce, after much hard detective work, everyone's favorite audience member, Eddie Krumble, The Clapper.

So here I am. It's all come to this. Incredible. I look out and wonder who's clapping for real, who's reading the prompter, who's being paid for this, giving their services away for free? Is Judy watching?

A million thoughts race through my mind but one mission. I'm here to find someone that makes me feel like someone's out there. I'm here to promote that.

First thing Jay wants to talk about is the ball-and-chain prop around my ankle. Some sort of joke or funny device Mr. Ranter (the producer) thought could help add some humor to the show. As if to say they finally caught me I guess. Seemed the audience found it funny for a moment as well. Fine with me. This is entertainment after all.

He begins the interview, or whatever you want to call it, asking questions he knows the answers to. I pick up we're supposed to act as if we hadn't already met. The meeting in the free sushi room will go unmentioned. I get it. Yeah, sure call me what you want. Eddie, Clapper, whatever. I'm here for Judy.

From sitting in the audience through hundreds of these shows I've learned people have to get straight and to the point. Get as much information out as you can before they cut to a commercial.

Fearing my time is limited I take in a deep breath as he asks about Judy. In one long exhaled run-on I blurt that I'm . . . here to find her cuz she got fired from this gas station and we were supposed to have this other date and I have no way of getting in touch with her so I came on here to promote her because I know you only pay guests by promoting them so I came here to promote that I was looking for Judy. That's her name, Judy.

Jay sits and does that talk show host funny extended silent stare. Audience cracks up. I don't care, I got it out.

He asks a few questions about Judy as I begin to see a curve in the interview. An unexpected turn. A detour.

People begin laughing at things there's no humor in. I mention she worked at a gas station. Laughter. Went to Astro Burger. Laughter. It's becoming a little unsettling. Knowing how quickly things can go from weird to worse I go silent.

And then it happened.

AUDIENCE MEMBER (*yells out*)
Give us a clap!

One after another. A chant is growing. Sporadic comments from all corners of the room provoke visions of Salem witch trials in me. "Give us a clap!" "Eddie The Clapper!" Applause. Laughter. Whistling. Try to ignore it as it grows louder. Jay Leno then pops the cork. Asks (very talk show host–like), "And about this well, clapping-type occupation you seem to be spearheading. Like how does one go about doing this for a job?"

I remind him that "one" is usually in hell when they do this type of job. "One" does not spearhead a situation like this. "One" is tired of being hooked up to intravenous for cash when "one" does this.

This has the audience falling out of their seats. Seems the more irate I become the more entertaining I become. My tolerance for humiliation directly linked to the funny meter.

The interview has now switched from promoting my search for Judy, to being a Clapper, to being tarred and feathered in front of millions of people. I'm a cartoon whose head explodes.

I keep going back to Judy but all anyone wants is for me to basically clap. How could this be entertaining? Do they expect to hear some incredible sound come from it? A new form of clap?

Every angle I turn leads to court jester. We discuss my being hooked up to an adrenaline drip and the audience goes hysterical. When I explain how it makes you anxious, it's as if Don Rickles is up there. What did they expect an adrenaline drip directly attached to a main artery to do?

Aside from Clapping, Jay's intrigued by the human research me and Chris used to do back in New York. Another obstacle now further separating the possibility of this interview being at all about finding Judy.

Jay's particularly interested in how we pretended to be doctors. I told him we'd put on scrubs, maybe a stethoscope, answer a few questions about oh I don't know . . . like what amount of cc's of like some cancer drug we'd admit some guy with like cancer or something and get paid.

I get one of those "*oohs*" from the audience as if I was affecting cancer in some way. When I asked Jay if they just put up a sign asking the audience to "*ooh*" they're back to laughing.

I explain that everyone at these test centers knows we aren't doctors. All just making a buck ya know? A bunch of baloney. Tell him I'm much happier being a Clapper.

He asks for a sample. Audience goes wild. I see this happen to different people on television. That actor Cuba Gooding can't seem to go anywhere without someone insisting he repeat that God-awful phrase "Show me the money!" Must hate that. I guess I can relate. Just take away the pay and any remnants of decency.

Jay requests a clap again.

I question what this would accomplish to the tune of an audience hanging on my every affliction. My body language involuntarily put its hands together in a sort of half-clap motion. The power of suggestion I guess.

Brought the whole place to its feet Clapping along. You'd of thought the Beatles had entered Shea Stadium.

This is insane! The more I questioned it the more they reacted.

Chants of "one more time" "C-L-A-P!" flutter the studio and my head. Someone screams for an "encore!"

An encore of what?

Jay defends the madness by stating that I've got to understand, to most people this "isn't say, the norm, as far as employment goes."

I remind him that unfortunately no one is "employing" me to sit in his seat and interview "one's spearheading" this occupation! Audience gives another unanimous "*ooooh*."

Noticing my irritation, Jay assures me we're all friends. That no one is attacking me.

I remind him the city is full of unflattering twenty-foot freeze-frame billboards of me with two hands about to meet in a clap that his show posted up. Next time you have a camera take a photo of yourself clapping and see how cool you look!

I get up to storm off and trip over the ball-and-chain prop. Audience is having the time of their lives. Backstage Ralph Ranter tries a, "they're loving you out there." I remind him if I were on fire they'd love me even more.

Didn't realize a camera followed me all the way out to the street where I had a screaming match with the show's lawyer (Horatio). He wears a top hat, holds a cane, sports a tuxedo (really), and a Colonel Sanders white handlebar mustache. Unbeknownst to me, a live broadcast of me telling Ranter to "get this fucking (beep) Monopoly-looking guy the hell away from me!" aired on that same show.

After a brief joke about the possible unsettling side effects of adrenaline testing, Jay turns his attention to the lawyer.

JAY LENO
Did he actually call you the Monopoly guy?

LAWYER GUY (Horatio)
I think he did.

AUDIENCE LAUGHTER

JAY LENO
I have to say Horatio, I do see a resemblance.

Tuesday. Explaining fraudulent cancer studies.

Tuesday morning. One week since I've last seen Judy. One night since my televised crucifixion. Twelve hours to my tentative date with Judy.

Last plan we had was to meet again tonight. Same place. Astro Burger. Lunch at 11 PM. My last chance to find her.

A calendar on the wall is full of Xs. Six for the past six days. Regressively becoming more and more faint. Defeated. Barely pushing ink to the page the past two. They are sad Xs but today brings hope. Today has a big circle around it. Made that circle last Wednesday. Couldn't wait.

Reality is always a knock away. Mine is a LOUD one.

VOICE

Edward . . . Edward Krumble please open the door.

Through the peek hole it's a scene from a TV cop show. Not particularly scary. More *Dragnet*. Think *Matrix* meets Dan Akroid or Tom Arnold. Two men in suits notice my presence behind the door.

MAN #1

FDA, Mr. Krumble. Please open the door.

I open and look for the cameras. Some kind of skit or something I'm sure. Had just about enough of this. He explains they're with the Food and Drug Administration. They'd like to ask me a few questions. Sure, downtown right? I mean, being this is a skit why not just go as cliché as possible.

They assure me it isn't a gag. They're with the Food and Drug Administration.

Seems I ticked off a few people going on national television explaining how I was making important decisions about the future of cancer for $45. I repeatedly told them it was just a gig. Way to make a buck. Nobody takes any of it seriously anyway. They tell me it would be in my best interest to come with them where they could interview me for a while. Making a quick buck, gags, and cancer research seem to not be a favorable combination with the FDA.

My interview/interrogation is relentless. "What do you mean when you repeatedly tell these surveyors *it varies*?" "What varies?" "Do you realize partaking falsely in medical research is a federal offense?"

Didn't know it was illegal. Immoral I imagined. "They know we aren't really doctors."

Contrary to the *Tonight Show*'s audience reaction, the FDA found no humor in this at all.

Day turned to night. 9:30 they finally decided to let me go.

One-and-a-half hours to get back to Hollywood. To see Judy.

Tuesday night's long journey home.

Downtown Los Angeles at night looks like the world ended and nobody told you. *Escape from New York* meets the *Twilight Zone*. Zombies roam freely.

After my interrogation I head to the subway. Before moving to Los Angeles I'd heard they had them here. Used to think, who would ride a subway in a city that has earthquakes? Takes all of about two seconds before that question's answered for you downtown at night.

Public transportation here in general is a world unto itself. A third world. In New York, auto mechanics sit beside lawyers on trains. Hot dog Salesmen rub elbows with real estate tycoons. Maintenance workers alongside restauranteurs.

Public transportation here is a staple of your UN-success. A badge of your misfortunes. Proof you're in the dumps.

Busses drive by like moving displays of who to avoid. Failure caravans.

I head down the subway to buy a ticket from a machine. No token booth people here. Run by an honor system. Buy a ticket from a machine, walk on in. Run into a cop, he may or may not ask you to show it.

The machine is broke. Clock on the wall says 9:55. One hour and five minutes to get to Judy. Two trains and one bus to Santa Monica Blvd. I hear a train pulling in. I'll never make it across the street to the other machine in time.

Rush through the gate and I'm immediately approached by a police officer. Wants to see my ticket. Seems he knew the machine was broke. Patiently waiting like a spider to a fly. Brings me back to his parlor (behind a wall obstructing the view) where two other fare jumpers sit sulking.

I tell him what he already knows. The machine was broke. Tell him what he doesn't care to know. I'm in a rush to see a girl.

Train pulls away as he sits me on a bench. Takes his time. Clock reads 10 PM.

Just write me the ticket already.

Another guy hops the gate.

10:05.

A second train comes roaring in. I'm no more than five feet from where the doors will open. Next one won't come til at least 10:20.

I've never run from a cop. Can't miss Judy though.

As the cop heads towards the fare beater (away from me) the

train pulls in. Doors open. I'm filled with anxiety. He can't even see me from where he is. I'll have switched trains before he even realizes I'm gone.

Adrenaline kicks to overload as I go for it. Doors close behind me. Off I go. Gone. On my way. Safe.

In the blackness of the tunnel the train stops to a halt. Over the loudspeaker I barely make out that it'll "just be a m#@ (*crackle*)%# (*crackle*) while they (*crackle*)."

Conductor enters my car with a police officer holding a walkie-talkie. Mumbles something into it while looking at me. Over it I hear a reply. "Yes. Balding Caucasian, white shoes." I guess that's me.

Apprehended. Taken off the subway for my second interrogation of the evening.

After checking me out, (no warrants), he hands me what I'm sure is a HUGE ticket and sends me on my way.

I arrive at Astro Burger at 12:25 AM. One hour and twenty-five minutes late. Judy's nowhere to be found.

Risa Risa! The humor in Rorschach testing.

I'm distraught over Judy. Devastated. If there's an answer, a way to find her I'm nowhere near figuring it out.

My financial situation's gone from worse to impossible. The subway ticket just made even that worse. Impossible is coming. And unfortunately, making impossible worse again isn't an upgrade in reverse. WOW! That being said, I guess the appropriate way of putting this would be, impossible just became worser.

There's a time everyone has to step down. Athletes become coaches, TV stars do reality, Clappers go to Telemundito.

Telemundito is a Spanish television network that also hosts shows for Japan. Whole different story. American television can certainly get pretty freaky. Spanish and Asian are on an entirely different playing field. That special place where '50s wholesome slapstick meets sadistic medieval practices.

Not that their shows aren't already entertaining (I watched a man get stung by forty-seven scorpions for forty-seven dollars once) but they pay Clappers as well.

I don't speak a lick of Spanish but know *aplauda* to be "clap," *risa* is "laugh," and that's all they or we care about anyway.

All Telemundito productions use the same paid audiences. Seems Japanese Clappers are few and far between. Mexican shows pay $25. Japanese $35. Neither pay as well as American but they don't know me here and I need cash.

Being the shows shoot quicker (contestants can only stand so much pain) you can squeeze in quite a few once you show up. We're booked for four today. Three Mexican and one Japanese. That's $115.

Chris is a good friend and comes along. English, Spanish, Japanese makes no difference to us much anyway. Long as you understand the prompters.

It can get confusing at times. Last time we did a Japanese show, someone was crying hysterically and "RISA" kept popping up. Thought I was reading it wrong until everyone started laughing. Except, of course, the person crying. Different sense of humor they have over there I guess. Very Rorschach test-ish.

They'll do whatever they want to you.

Our first job of the day was a Mexican court show. Latin American television is like a mad chef who can't part with say, oregano. Sprinkles a little on everything. Replace oregano with giant breasts, some slapstick, and you get the idea.

EVERY show they do will include these very basic yet mandatory ingredients. It'll be like OK we'll do a court show but the stenographer will only wear a bra and just . . . I don't know, make someone fall and break their head open or something.

All I know is this court show was terrible. Couldn't understand one word but that translation was crystal clear.

Seems some poor guy was suing a horrible little store in Rancho Cucamonga about a rotten wig they sold him.

Way these shows work is as follows: devious and diligent producers from all over the world of reality and court TV dig through pending small claims case files open to the public. Looking, searching meticulously for the most God-awful lawsuits they can find.

Trust me. If you're suing your abusive husband for $35 because he slept with your sister and drank all your vodka, SOMEONE from television land will find you.

They'll offer both sides a no-lose situation. Sort of. Person suing, win or lose will get the $35 they're suing for. Being the show pays this settlement the defendant isn't at risk financially, either. Morally, ethically, and as far as being publicly humiliated throughout the eternity of reruns, an entirely different story. There is a price to be paid for everything.

American television has questionable morals as well but slightly tougher standards. This in no way reflects a more evolved society. Just one that has more lawyers prepared to sue over things. Asian and Latin American television, simply put, are the Old West with cameras.

On this show I pick up that one of the guys is suing over a $35 wig he felt made him look *"insensato"* (foolish). All of a sudden the producer calls "CUT!" A heated confrontation ensues as they try to convince the man to put the wig ON his head instead of holding it in his hand for demonstration (humiliating) purposes.

He looks distraught. Embarrassed. Doesn't want to wear it. Producer threatens him with no pay. *"Ningún dinero!"* He looks back, two, even three times to his wife. Over and over as if to say we need the money but this is humiliating.

Finally, he reluctantly, humbly, and timidly places it on his head as the cameras roll.

On cue the attorney defending the wig store theatrically RIPS it off and throws it to the ground.

Laughter sign goes off like an alarm. RISA RISA! Everyone, including me and Chris, laugh on cue. I watch the camera move in on the humiliated Mexican man slowly picking his wig up off the ground. He'll get his $35 now. We'll get our 25.

Walking out I tell Chris I felt bad for the guy. He tells me they'll do whatever they want to you. He's right.

We follow the sign towards our next gig. A Japanese game show. I ask someone to translate the name of it. *This* Was *Your Life*.

For $50 you wouldn't let us burn the skin off your feet right?

The $115 from Telemundito barely makes a dent in my situation. Actually none at all.

I wonder if Judy saw that episode of Jay Leno last week? Fantasize she was changing channels and landed right up on it. "What's Eddie doing on TV?"

I contact Ralph Ranter and agree to come on one last time. No funny business this time or I'm outta here. Really.

Next day I'm booked and back in the free green sushi room. Ranter assures me the interview will be geared around my search for Judy. Says to make myself comfortable, he'll be right back.

Whenever he steps out or asks me to hold a minute I get nervous. Ten thousand times bitten, twenty thousand shy. I'm no fool.

I no longer hesitate for some free sushi. Growing more comfortable in my role. Assertive in my mission.

Another guest sits across from me. Looks familiar. I tell him this whole ordeal makes me feel like Charlie Brown. That scene where Peppermint Patty tells him to kick the football and repeatedly moves it just before he gets there, landing him on his head. Guest corrects me that I'm referring to Lucy, not Peppermint Patty.

Forgetting, of course, these are cartoon characters, I ask if he knows them.

GUEST IN FREE-SUSHI ROOM
Well I know the cartoon Eddie. That is your name right? And it seems to me like you're letting Jay and all of *them* control *your* situation. Am I right?

I look again and notice the guest to be that self-help guru Tony Robbins. Guy's like seven feet tall. Tell him I actually did one of his shows a ways back. Paid well. Hundred and fifty dollars if I remember correctly. They had me walk on hot coals. A cinch being they weren't even hot.

TONY ROBBINS
Well of course they weren't hot. If they were you'd of burnt the skin off your feet. What that showed you was that *you* had the courage to do something you were afraid to do. That you were in charge. That you had faith I wouldn't let you burn the skin off your feet.

I reminded him they did pay $150 as well. He quickly added,

"Yes but you wouldn't let us burn the skin off your feet for $150 right?" I paused. Was that a question or an offer?

He gave me a quick self-help assurance pep talk. Something about taking control of a fishing line or . . . comparing me to a fish on a line or . . . I don't know. Sounded interesting. Those things always do. Actually almost bought a book of cassettes his show was pedaling that time til I realized I was about to buy a book of cassettes.

He told me not to let Jay take charge. Go on out there and be "in control."

As I sat wondering how to exactly take charge, how to get the conversation to just be about Judy, how . . . amazingly enormous Tony Robbins was (the guy is HUGE), they called me onto the show.

JAY LENO
And it's my extreme pleasure to once again bring on our
good friend Eddie Krumble, The Clapper. Eddie, c'mon
over here.

I walk out suspicious. Suspicious of every word Jay says. Knew the interview could turn on a dime. Seen it happen firsthand.

Too cautious, the place'll pick up on it. Too loose, worse. Frozen. Didn't expect it to be this bad. Feeling was that of smoking bad pot. Except that, yes, everyone in the place really is watching and laughing at me.

I cough, place goes hysterical, so I stop coughing. They (the audience) sense I didn't finish my cough. Only got half out. They know this. I know this and somehow this is even funnier. Chuckles become out and out laughter as Jay asks if I'd like some water.

He acknowledges my walking off the previous time. Afraid to cough or . . . not cough I don't answer. From the corner of my eye a camera slowly zooms in as the audience uncomfortably chuckles yet again.

Searching for a safe area to view I spot their lawyer, now FULLY dressed as the Monopoly Guy. Bait on a hook. Show can't wait for me to mention him. Camera on standby just dying to feature his funny little outfit on the screen. Maybe play back the taped argument between us in the street. I'm not biting.

Longer I stared the harder it was to even blink. The more impossible it became. I could hear laughter but it sounded a million miles away. Camera closing in. I mumble out an apology for walking off. Jay says there's no need and goes directly to Judy (a promise kept).

Judy. The magic word. Yes, that's why I was there. Here.

My mind always races. I go through a whole gamut of useless data whenever I try and get a thought out. Yes, Judy. I was almost home-free until I glanced back over at that Monopoly lawyer again. Get out of jail free, Boardwalk, Park Place, B & O Railroad.

Why did I have to mention that last time? Everything was suddenly a giant Monopoly set. Like a quiet fit of torrents I involuntarily gurgle out "Boardwalk." Jay Leno asks why I said that as that camera on standby flashes to the lawyer. Place goes nuts.

I've had about enough. "What do you want me to clap?" Place is in an uproar as I stand and yell to the audience. Gorilla's outta the cage. Stupid Pet Trick gone wrong. Trained genius pig booked to recite alphabet instead urinates on host's leg. EVEN BETTER! The late great Brother Theodore once said, "I should have known better than to try and sell roses in a fish market."

Was at a loss as to what to do. If I left again my hopes of ever finding Judy would leave along with me.

I looked at Jay and told him it didn't matter. Sat back down. They could laugh all they wanted. All night if they wanted. Didn't matter one bit. I was there to find Judy. This was my best and last hope.

I explained there weren't enough hours in the night when she was around. My nights and days had now become endless.

Didn't occur to me I was even on national television anymore. Judy was gone. The world was empty.

Jay asked for a description. Long brown hair, beautiful in a kind of unbeautiful way.

Suddenly I was out of the trance. Back on television. Place was silent. Jay cleared his throat. "This Judy must be quite a girl to have made such an impact on you." Audience slowly fades in with applause that seems genuine.

Tell him this show was my only hope. My last hope. I was there to promote my search for Judy.

JAY LENO
Well we did find you didn't we?

The audience wakes up with applause. Jay looks into the camera and gives a direct order to his viewing audience.

JAY LENO
OK, we know her name is Judy, she's got long brown

hair. She's beautiful in a kind of unbeautiful way, right? She was recently fired from a gas station on Santa Monica Boulevard and we need you to help us find her!

Backstage I couldn't have been happier. Broke, unemployed, a wreck, but word was out. Ralph Ranter rushed over to commend me on an incredible appearance and offered me a job.

Seems it went so well they'd like to send me out on the streets doing some skits. In the vein of the ones Jay did when looking for me. "Jaywalking" ones.

They're gonna send me out with pay to look for Judy.

Eddie out on the streets.

They're calling the segments "Eddie Out on the Streets." Me and Chris roaming around Hollywood looking for Judy. Chris is sort of my Ed McMahon and I'm sort of . . . the guy who walks around the streets. Don't know how many we'll do but agree on $2,000 apiece each time we do it.

First place I'm sent is the gas station. Haseem Karesh is back in the box. I tell Ranter it'll be a waste of time. As we know, Haseem speaks English payment methods only. Won't be of much help locating Judy. They insist we try.

To no surprise Haseem rattles off a long list of acceptable credit options. Lets us know checks will not be accepted as suddenly the naked man runs by. I tell them Judy knew him. "That's Naked Larry."

Ranter and the audience eat this up. They're calling me a gold mine. The new Larry Bud Melman. Ratings are through the roof.

In the first week we appear on the show four separate nights. Money's coming in. Words getting out. Still no sign of Judy.

Sasquatch.

I'm called in for a studio appearance on the show. Funny how things have changed. I come out to a loud round of applause and sit across from Jay. Monopoly lawyer guy (in full getup) walks over to present my check for the week's work. It's all a big skit but I'm getting paid and hopefully closer to finding Judy.

Jay asks I take a look at something on the monitor.

Fuzzy footage of Judy walking out to replace a gas pump appears. It's from about six months ago. Filmed by the station's surveillance camera. Jay appropriately compares it to Bigfoot footage as he introduces a special guest, Haseem Karesh.

Seems after my riveting interview with Haseem the other day, Ralph Ranter approached and discussed his appearing on the show. Can't imagine what they spoke about but have a pretty good idea money came into the discussion.

Leave it to Ranter though. Man could negotiate with a hungry bear.

Haseem walks out proud as a peacock. After Jay gets a lesson in currency and miscommunication I take over the interview. If anyone knows where she is, it's him. Locked somewhere inside this linguistic money riddle has got to at least be an address, number, or last name.

Where's Judy? Over and over again his answer is simply, "Yes. I'm fired her."

I can't take it anymore and go at him. Jay pulls us apart. Cuts to a commercial.

Backstage we gather Judy was working off the books and neither Hassem nor the station has any further information.

A break.

Next day I'm called in again. Seems an intern followed up on a lead and Judy's been contacted. She's a bit confused but agreed to speak with me on air.

JAY LENO

So let's patch her in then. Hello Judy is that you?

JUDY

Eddie? What's going on? I had about ten different people on the street say they saw me, and now these people are calling and . . . Eddie. Is that you?

I'm beside myself. Told her not to worry, it's only Jay Leno. She's confused. Jay chimes in there's nothing to be afraid of. When she asks who he is, the audience laughs. When she asks who's laughing they laugh harder. I'm seeing where this can go and I don't like it. This is the moment of truth. My chance and I'm not gonna allow it to become another skit.

Judy, don't worry. I've just been looking for you and . . .

Before I finish she says something that will change everything. Didn't even notice it at the time. Just a simple word said in confusion.

JUDY
And I don't even know if this is you. This could be some
kind of stalker or . . . this is weird. I think I have to hang up.

No. Wait!

She hung up and all I could think of was getting her back on the line. Her using the word "stalker" didn't even phase me.

Backstage Ranter was in a panic yelling for his intern to get her back on the line.

If they'll just give me her number I know I can straighten this out. They say she only gave permission to talk that one time. That they couldn't give her number out.

Permission? These are the guys who filled Los Angeles with twenty-foot billboards of me looking like an idiot. Basically outed me as a paid audience member and now they're concerned about "permission"!

Ranter jumps in to defuse the situation. Tells me to let them work on it for the day and they're sure it'll be fine.

I have no choice.

The thin line between Don Juan and Jack the Ripper.

Back when Chris smoked a lot of pot he once said it was a thin line between Don Juan and Jack the Ripper. All the romantic notions of fighting for the girl who doesn't want you, being persistent, winning her over had been ruined by that simple buzzword "stalker." I stood dumbfounded. He fell asleep and forgot he said it.

Yeah, stalking someone is awful but I mean, we grew up on the idea a little stalking could be sort of romantic. Remember a movie once where some guy won the heart of a girl who found him repulsive by filling her entire front lawn with red roses. Sounds like a felony.

Take *Sleepless in Seattle* for instance. Meg Ryan uses her

privileges as a journalist to uncover personal information about Sam (Tom Hanks). She then hires a private investigator to follow him, map out his daily routine, and take pictures of him. This is all done in a way that makes her seem like a lovelorn romantic. She is, after all, Meg Ryan. Take a few teeth out, put some dirty clothes on her, and we're talking a whole other film. One I'd probably enjoy a whole lot more.

My search for Judy was innocent. Persistent, yes. Malicious, never.

The day after my last appearance on Jay Leno I woke up to a story on some morning talk show.

Between the landlord banging and those relentless barking dogs down the hall I could barely make out what they were saying. A freeze-frame of myself accompanied by one of the girls on this show saying, "something about that guy always gave her the creeps anyway" led me to believe it was probably not a complimentary piece.

Tried to get more but the banging wouldn't stop. Landlord was there for the rent. He called the last two days but my phone was turned off. Handed him a check as I ran back to the TV.

Story wrapped up with, "Hey, one day you're the hero, next day . . . well in further and slightly more newsworthy stories . . ."

I grabbed my umbrella and headed out to the phone company.

The telephone company.

Phone company offices, hospital emergency rooms, and DMVs are endless waiting grounds. Even have areas sectioned off for this particular service (waiting rooms). Built solely for the purpose of having people "wait." Quite Seinfeld-ish huh? But really, if Purgatory is ever proven to be on this earth, these three places most certainly should be investigated.

Every few minutes I step out to a public phone. Call in to see if the show wants me there. A skit, an interview, any word on Judy?

Back and forth from the pay phone, Ranter is unavailable. Strange. He's always been available before.

What I didn't know was an emergency staff meeting had been called at NBC studios. A whole team of irate producers were there to confront Ralph Ranter.

One throws down the day's *Daily News*. Headline reads:

Jay Leno Accused of Aiding Stalker!

Ralph attempts to calm them down. Says Judy was confused and the papers are running with it. Reminds them Eddie's (I'm) a fan favorite. That they were all fine moving along with the segments. An executive producer guy saw it quite differently while yelling that Ranter and Horatio (Monopoly lawyer guy) had put Jay Leno's reputation at stake.

Ralph repeats that I'm not a stalker. That Judy just dropped the word in confusion. A big misunderstanding. They're overreacting.

EXECUTIVE MAX

Overreacting? We've got newspapers circulating stories convicting Jay of aiding a stalker. Do you find that something not to be overreacting to? Public opinion is about to convict our host of a felony! What we have to do is find some kind of way to right this wrong. And as for our Clapper segments . . . bury them. Never existed far as I'm concerned.

While this is going on I'm still at the telephone company. Completely ignorant to the disaster brewing.

Sitting in one of those long rows of orange plastic chairs all attached to each other watching a crappy wall-mounted television. Larry King show's on. Through the blurry static I make out that same frozen image of myself. Says something across me . . . not Clapper. Alleg . . ? . . . Alliga . . . tor? Allegations, that's it. STALKER ALLEGATIONS!!??

Just to the side is . . . Chris talking with Larry King! Jump onto my seat to get a better view. Oh my God. It is Chris!

LARRY KING (on TV)

We have here, in the studio with us Chris Plork. You may remember Chris as the man who originally helped lead Jay Leno to the now-notorious, Eddie The Clapper. Hello Chris.

CHRIS (on TV)

Hello.

LARRY KING (on TV)

Now, Chris do you find your friend Eddie to be dangerous in any way?

CHRIS (on TV)

Well . . .

PSYCHOLOGIST GUEST (on TV)

Larry, often stalkers aren't harmful at all. They're just lonely people who latch on to someone who just, well, gives them any kind of attention.

LARRY KING (on TV)

OK, Chris, would you consider your friend Eddie to be a lonely type of guy?

CHRIS (on TV)

We're all kind of lonely I guess.

LARRY KING (on TV)
Yes, but we all don't go on national television to stalk someone who gave us a little bit of attention. And may I add, we did try and contact The Clapper directly but it seems his phone has been disconnected.

PSYCHOLOGIST GUEST (on TV)
That's a common trait. They will go underground or lay dormant as we sometimes say for extended periods of time before resurfacing and . . .

I ran the hell out and back to that pay phone outside. Appropriately it begins to pour. I insist they put Ralph Ranter on as he picks up.

Fully aware of the situation he insists everything will be fine. Just wants to be sure I don't have any kind of criminal past or anything. Of course not! Didn't even want any of this! They were the ones that did this. They put me all over the TV. All over the city. You did this to me Ralph!

Talk shows are saying I'm laying dormant. Gone underground. I'm beside myself. If he'll just give me Judy's number I know I can straighten this whole thing out.

Tells me that's COMPLETELY out of the question. Hangs up as I cling to the pay phone like a pacifier. Security blanket, life raft. Immobile once again.

A car drives by. Two young girls from inside yell they love me. I look up and realize I'm directly below a billboard of myself. This would probably be quite funny if it wasn't the worst thing in the world.

Months later.

For months I've watched that first billboard on Santa Monica Blvd. of me change. A slight tear in the corner of what's now a Coca-Cola ad reveals remnants of my hand in mid-clap.

I've seen Judy 10,000 times since. Supermarkets, movie theaters, 7-11's, everywhere. I get close enough and the image changes. It's not her.

Wake up every day with her on my mind. Every day there's hope. Engage in a conversation and over the person's shoulder there she'll be. Then gone.

I'm a shadow of a man who was not much more than a shadow to start with. A walking sad sack.

It's been a hard four months. The show stopped calling me and eventually I stopped calling them. Held out an entire month waiting for that ring acknowledging it all as a big misunderstanding. It never came.

My star has faded. Potion exposed. Bubble gum popped.

I'm back working marketing research now. Me and Chris. My good and loyal friend. Nothing too interesting. Blindfolded Coke versus Pepsi things ya know? Oh, it's Coke! Wow, I usually drink Pepsi.

A void I never knew existed now exists. Judy's gone.

I have an agent now. Jeffrey George. Made an exception to the "no dealings with people with two first names" rule me and Chris always had, due to the fact it was either him or . . . no one.

JG (that's what he calls himself) is sort of the low-end of low-end almost-had-beens.

Sounds awful but occasionally he'll get me a job paying a few hundred bucks. Just last week I was clapping (yes clapping) at a new Target Store in Redondo Beach. And yes, that IS as terrible as it sounds. Gotta make a living though.

If you believe in fate then all things lead to clapping in Redondo Beach. If it's reincarnation, my previous lives have been narrowed down to either Nazi soldier or really good bug.

The *Tom and Emma Show*

Jeffrey George (JG) booked me on the *Tom and Emma Show*. A husband/wife talk show in the vein of oh, you know? Crap. Plays every other Monday on like channel one million sixty-seven.

Occasionally I'll get booked on a few of these terrible shows as they go down their long laundry list of unanswered guest invitations. I imagine my name being somewhere between the expired cast of *Eight Is Enough* and that monkey on skates. Yeah, that one. Right there. Back and forth. Back and forth.

So here I am on any other Monday sitting in the green room (this one is more a mustard yellow) of the *Tom and Emma Show*.

Actually watched this one a few times on extremely depressed and unemployed afternoons. So absolutely horrendous eventually you just phase it out. No need to shut it off. It's just not there. Wholesome family sludge.

Watched them for an entire hour once talk enthusiastically about the importance of choosing the right POTHOLDERS! No joke. An hour! On and on. Occasionally I'd see the husband (Tom) look off to the side. Probably a clock, producer, or flash at how his life had become so successfully mundane.

In the mustard yellow room I recognize all Jeffrey George's fellow clients. My peers. Spinning-plate guy, kid who tampered with a foul ball during a World Series game (3 YEARS AGO), all of them. Us. Ugh.

Occasionally you'll catch a glimpse of the superstars of this awful circuit. Dr. Ruth Westheimer (sex therapist from the '80s), Corey Feldman, the "adopted" Brady kid. Never know whether to acknowledge or just pretend you don't recognize the ugly hand fate's dealt them.

To put it bluntly, this circuit is so low, reality TV isn't even interested in making you eat bugs.

Infamous and infamy can be perfectly defined in one quick scope of the mustard yellow room.

Look around and realize I'm only looking inward. A horrible conceded understanding blankets me as the Tom Cruise look-alike practice his *Risky Business* moves in a dirty mirror. Before I can get any more reflective in this celebrity septic tank, I'm called in.

Come out to an audience of Clappers. For a second I actually see that sort of excitement in their eyes. Unsure exactly how they know me. Get that a lot these days. Quickly turns to a smirk, laugh, and then, whisper. Saw it happen to Eric Estrada once but people actually did love him at one time. Grew up with him on their television sets. Mothers and grandmothers had schoolgirl crushes on him. Little boys wanted to be Ponch. I'm a different case. A momentary joke. Human banana peel tripping up that monkey on skates. Yeah, that one.

Tom and Emma (husband/wife talk show hosts) introduce me, "You must remember him, the world's most famous Clapper!"

I watch the Clappers go back to their routines as I'm greeted by Tom and Emma. This must be the twentieth time I've done this. They'll ask where I've been and I'll answer that I've been on all the other shows that ask me that same question. Audience will laugh because it seems this is my niche. Cynicism. They enjoy my bitterness. I prefer to call it straightforwardness.

If I'm honest they'll laugh, if I'm quiet they'll laugh, if they don't think I'm funny the prompter will tell them to laugh and they will. It can be overwhelming. An endless three-dimensional laugh track surrounds me.

I start the interview asking why the "Oatmeal Guy" . . . yeah, he's back in the mustard yellow room. Why he's getting a thousand dollars for his appearance while I'm only getting $700.

It seems oatmeal guy was kicked off one of those *Survivor*-type shows (you never heard of) two years ago and has recently joined us in this incredible journey DOWN the stairway FROM the stars.

His "thing," or claim to fame, was that he ALWAYS ate oatmeal. Fascinating, huh? Probably not, I imagine. But the last laugh, it seems, is on all of us, being Quaker Oats signed him to some phenomenal deal just to mention that not only does he eat oatmeal but Quaker Oats is his choice amongst oatmeals. So many angles. How is anyone broke?

Tom and Emma aren't particularly interested in discussing Oatmeal Guy's appearance wages with me. Mine or anyone else's for that matter. Why would they when there are so many other interesting topics to tackle? I'm talking they actually mentioned how different cultures clap in different ways. Obviously had some poor intern research this all day.

Did you know it was improper etiquette to clap in most Asian countries? Of course not. WHO THE HELL CARES?

Once they finally exhausted every aspect of the variations of applauding (those variations when broken down basically being loud and soft) they steered off course to ask what ever happened to Judy. Before I can reply someone in the studio audience stands up.

AUDIENCE MEMBER
If you wanted to see me then why didn't you come to Astro Burger?

Tom and Emma jump as if someone's fired a shot. God forbid a moment of spontaneity. All I heard was this person say "me" instead of "her."

The audience member continues standing. It's Judy!

JUDY
I was there. I waited an hour. Then I gave up and you went on this whole crazy TV thing. Why would you do that to me? You made a big joke out of us and then you disappeared.

I couldn't believe my eyes and certainly not my ears. Actually almost fainted.

Along with everyone in that studio, Tom and Emma were at a loss for words.

I jumped to tell her after she was fired I had no way of getting in touch with her. Knew it was crazy to go on Jay Leno but didn't know what else to do. That they could do what they wanted with me. Put me in a gorilla suit for all I cared. Just needed to find her.

In a moment out of, well . . . nothing I can think of she started walking towards me. Not a producer, security guard, or host on this earth could have stopped it.

A camera swung to follow her every move. She hesitated. Made her uncomfortable. Told her to forget that stuff. It'll drive ya nuts if you let it.

She hesitantly walked up as I stepped down. We met and hugged on national television amidst a sea of Clappers breaking slowly, voluntarily, and vehemently into a standing ovation. Then and there I told her I didn't wanna spend another minute without her. No more spaceships Judy. Not without you.

Dropped to one knee and asked her to marry me.

A catatonic Tom and Emma were led over by their producer who offered us a new kitchen and dinette set. We accepted, as I placed my old high school Co-op ring on her finger.

Fame. The good kind.

By the time we arrived home Tiffany jewelers had offered any ring on the house. Endorsements were flying in through the doors. Offers to appear on every major network show were pouring in. Jeffrey George (JG) mentioned talks of our own husband and wife talk show. Every news program there we were.

ANCHORMAN #1 (V.O.)

In what has got be one of the strangest reunions in television history, the normally Nielsen-ly challenged Tom and Emma show had a moment that will go down in reality history today!

Switch to any channel and they were talking about it.

ANCHORMAN JOHN

. . . and are expecting a 26-point share. Somewhere in
the world of a 17.2 rating on the rebroadcast which will
air this Friday. Wow!

MTV ANCHOR GIDEON YAGO

. . . and as if that weren't enough it seems plans are
already in the works for none other than a reality show
chronicling the lives of America's latest infectious duo.

The magazine racks were full of nothing but flattering photographs of me and Judy. Turn on the radio and there we were again.

NEWS RADIO (V.O.)

Famed television . . . audience member Edward
Krumble and renowned missing gas station attendant
Judith Lettingo have announced plans for a June wedding. This comes on the announcement of a six-figure
publishing deal for an upcoming book entitled *Clapping All the Way to The Bank* which in Krumble's
words touches on "all kinds of things and stuff."

Our marriage took place live on the Jay Leno show and was
the highest-rated single episode of any talk show. Beating out Tiny
Tim and Miss Vicki's wedding back in 1969.

JAY LENO

They said it would never happen ladies and gentleman.
Eddie Krumble and the lovely Judy Lettingo!

Everything you never dreamed of.

Over the years me and Judy will have three kids, Dinicious (like my grandfather), Brian (as in Wilson), and Judy.

We'll open our lifelong dream:

EDDIE (THE CLAPPER) and JUDY'S BETA ONLY VIDEO & PET STORE!

Yeah, I stuck "THE CLAPPER" on it cuz it seems to bring people in. Chris, of course, is a partner. He eventually married the counter lady, Rita, from Astro Burger and they have a daughter (Pabuelita).

On the opening day of our lifelong dream the Jay Leno show came to film it.

For extra money on the side we'll do appearances in strange places over the next few years as our star slowly and happily fades back to quiet as opposed to oblivion.

Ring Inn the New Year with Eddie (The Clapper) and Judy Krumble at the Valley Forge Inn! Midnight champagne toast! Hottest ticket inn the valley!

The Valley in Los Angeles loves the play on words. ("Inn" the Valley.)

We work, me, Judy, Chris, Rita, Dinicious, Brian, Little Judy, and Pabuelita as a family. An unbreakable chain at the video and pet store. It does OK but we do better.

So in a story (my story) that at one time could have been wrapped up simply by the fact that I use the word *well* a lot. Actually no ones really can.

But because I did believe that at one time, I feel obligated to try and end this one with it. *Hmmmm.*

OK, how about, well, these days Edward Krumble (me) is doing quite well.